D0261414

PENGUIN BOOKS

Ruby Red

Praise for *The Year the Gypsies Came*:

'Wonderful . . . This is a new book with an old and wise heart. It may very well have the makings of a classic' *Guardian*

'Beautifully, powerfully and compellingly written . . . extraordinarily moving' *Sunday Times*

'This outstanding first novel arcs beautifully to its terrible climax and is deeply moving' *Observer*

'A beautifully evoked, exquisitely written novel' *Sunday Telegraph*

'A gripping read from an exciting new author' *Independent*

'Realistically evoking the perspective of a child of the era, Glass spins a lyrical story that is at once heart-breaking and hopeful' *Time Out*

'Every now and then a book comes along that's unusual, compelling and deeply absorbing yet is so tragically simple, it leaves an indelible trace on the memory. *The Year the Gypsies Came* is one of these' *Irish Independent*

'Unputdownable' *Telegraph*

Books by Linzi Glass

THE YEAR THE GYPSIES CAME
RUBY RED

Ruby Red

LINZI GLASS

PENGUIN BOOKS

This book is dedicated to thirteen-year-old Hector Pieterson, the first child to be killed on 16 June 1976, and to all the children who lost their lives during the Soweto Riots.

PENGUIN BOOKS

Published by the Penguin Group
Penguin Books Ltd, 80 Strand, London WC2R ORL, England
Penguin Group (USA) Inc., 375 Hudson Street, New York, New York 10014, USA
Penguin Group (Canada), 90 Eglinton Avenue East, Suite 700, Toronto, Ontario, Canada M4P 2Y3
(a division of Pearson Penguin Canada Inc.)
Penguin Ireland, 25 St Stephen's Green, Dublin 2, Ireland (a division of Penguin Books Ltd)
Penguin Group (Australia), 250 Camberwell Road, Camberwell, Victoria 3124, Australia
(a division of Pearson Australia Group Pty Ltd)
Penguin Books India Pvt Ltd, 11 Community Centre, Panchsheel Park, New Delhi – 110 017, India
Penguin Group (NZ), 67 Apollo Drive, Rosedale, North Shore 0632, New Zealand
(a division of Pearson New Zealand Ltd)
Penguin Books (South Africa) (Pty) Ltd, 24 Sturdee Avenue, Rosebank, Johannesburg 2196, South Africa

Penguin Books Ltd, Registered Offices: 80 Strand, London WC2R ORL, England

penguin.com

First published 2007
1

Text copyright © Linzi Glass, 2007

Set in Sabon by Palimpsest Book Production Limited, Grangemouth, Stirlingshire
Made and printed in England by Clays Ltd, St Ives plc

British Library Cataloguing in Publication Data
A CIP catalogue record for this book is available from the British Library

HARDBACK
ISBN: 978–0–141–38280–7

TRADE PAPERBACK [OM]
ISBN: 978–0–141–38281–4

'Art is the blood of a nation.
Stop the arteries and the heart will die'
Linda Givon, owner of the Goodman Gallery,
Johannesburg/Cape Town, South Africa

Chapter One

I remember the first time I heard my mother mention Julian Mambasa. 'His work is astounding. It cut right through me, made me almost gasp out aloud,' she told Father and me after her first meeting with Julian. It was at an underground art exhibit in Braamfontein, the part of town where respectable seventeen-year-old young ladies like me were never allowed to go.

My mother, Annabel, owned one of the most well-known art galleries in Johannesburg. It was also one of the most controversial. The gallery carried the works of both the famous and infamous and the serene walls were hung with paintings of both the struggling and the successful. Talent, Mother always said, knew no boundaries.

In the past Mother had helped starving artists with money and supplies, but she had been so appalled to learn that Julian painted in his dimly lit shanty in Soweto that it didn't take much for her to convince Father to let him move his meagre supplies, broken easel and tattered paintbrushes to our guest house. Airy and spacious, it had once been used entirely as a playroom for me, their only child.

On the first day that Julian arrived he was overwhelmed by what he saw.

'Madam Annabel, you shouldn't have, really you are much too kind, too kind . . .' He had lowered his head and placed his large hands across his heart.

Mother had gone out and bought him the finest brushes, a gleaming new easel and beautifully fine stretched canvases.

'Aah, but your talent deserves this,' was all she said.

Her name had been well chosen for it meant beauty and grace. She was fair haired and slight with a slender boyish figure that gave her the advantage of wearing flimsy dresses that hung perfectly on her slender hips. I had inherited none of her pale fragility. I was already taller than her with dark hair and eyes and an athletic frame that served me well on the school track team.

I had stood silently beside Mother, feeling surprisingly shy in front of Julian. Mother had not told me that he was barely in his twenties, which made him just a few years older than me.

'Ruby,' he had said when Mother had introduced us. 'Madam Annabel, you did not tell me that you hide your most valued masterpiece at home.'

I had waited to hear him laugh at his joke but saw only warm dark eyes looking down at me.

It was May 1976 and South Africa was at the height of apartheid, where the laws of segregation were strictly enforced. A harsh, unforgiving and hateful time when blacks and whites were forbidden to share the same public bench let alone share a meal together. It was on that crisp, cold day in May that my friendship with Julian Mambasa began. Ours was a bond that could not exist beyond the gates of our hilltop home in the affluent, white suburb of Westcliff.

But friendship, much like talent, knows no boundaries.

Julian arrived each morning on a bus marked in big black letters, NON-WHITES/*NIE BLANKES*, that dropped him off at the bottom of the hill on Jan Smuts Avenue. From here he would dodge his way through busy morning traffic, stopping briefly to buy a morning copy of the *Rand Daily Mail* newspaper from the young *piccanin* with the runny nose and tattered clothes that were two sizes too big for him.

'I am a lucky one. Lucky to have met such a good woman as your mother,' Julian told me as he set up his new easel to begin his day's work of painting and sketching in the quiet of a clean bright studio.

He shook his head as he looked around the dazzling studio. 'This is nothing like my home.'

I found myself drawn to the studio every day after school. Between brush strokes I learned about his life in Soweto, how he would wake up every morning to the raspy squawking of his neighbour Phillamon's chickens. He would sneak into their yard and dig for his morning's breakfast of eggs from under their warm feathers.

'A hen is a good thing to own in Soweto. Guarantee of food. Better than some who have to go to the garbage dumps to find scraps to feed themselves and their young.'

3

Julian painted the view through his cracked, small window in his works: a washing line being hung by a crooked, wrinkled old woman with a basket balancing on her wobbly head, a broken bottle in the hands of a scarred young *tsotsie* outside a *shebeen*, a makeshift drinking parlour, a mother with big melancholy eyes feeding her baby in the gutter outside the one free clinic near Baragwanath Hospital, an outhouse, rust-covered pipes leaking stinking water where a ten-year-old boy slept with his head in the filth. This was the view from Julian's room in Soweto.

While the view from my bedroom was of lush gardens, at a tender age my parents had shown me that the world we lived in was wrong – that people shouldn't have to live in separate areas or ride in separate buses or be treated differently because of the colour of their skin. But by lifting the veil of ignorance from my young eyes they created another kind of division. They separated me from my peers, for I lived in a hidden world that existed behind our large iron gates. Here in the safety and privacy of our home, people were treated as if colour didn't matter. Underground meetings of the illegal African National Congress were held sometimes in the late hours of the night, where Father was often the only white person present. Afternoon teas were served amongst the burnished orange geraniums that lined the finely manicured lawns to Mother's liberal art-loving crowd where Xhosa and Zulu were spoken as frequently as English over just-baked crumpets and scones. The ever-present threat that a raid by police could turn our world upside down in an instant forced me into a life of even greater secrecy at school. What happened at home was to stay at home. But we did not realize then that our iron gates could not keep out the hate.

'It's the splinters of glass in people's eyes that makes them see the world in jagged little pieces. If we could just get the glass out we could make them see clearly.'

My father often quoted from *The Snow Queen* to me. It was his favourite children's story and he had been telling it to me since I was five. I think my father, David, always the idealist, expected to represent only good people with honest problems when he became a partner in a very important law firm, but he soon discovered that there were many unsavoury characters he was made to represent. Getting the crooked rich off was not his idea of being a lawyer, so he began seeking cases to help the disenfranchised blacks. It helped him feel as if he were making a difference, that all those years of studying had not been for nothing.

My father had thick wavy black hair and a muscular frame. He had large thick-fingered hands that he used with purpose. He never spoke down to anyone. Everyone counted. He loved the story of the Snow Queen because it was a quest about setting a wrong right. He told me this tale over and over again as I sat in my fluffy bunny slippers and drank hot frothy milk in his oversized leather chair in his warm study.

Julian's favourite book was *Harold and the Purple Crayon*. He explained it all to me during one of our many afternoons together in the crisp white studio where he painted or sketched in charcoal.

'I hear this story when I was just a small *piccanin*; it was being read by a white madam to her little boy. Me, I was there to help my mother fold up the many piles of laundry. Mama, she was working then as washerwoman for Dr and Mrs Gordon in a big house in Hyde Park three days a week.'

Between the folds of the warm sheets the words of Harold reached him. With his purple crayon in his small hand, Harold drew his world and then stepped into it. A path, an apple tree, even a whole city full of windows.

'See, Harold, he created his own truth. You understand? He made it as nice and as comfortable as he liked. He drew things that could make a problem go away, and – *puff* – no problem any more.'

I nodded even though I wasn't too sure what Julian meant.

'See, Ruby, if there was a big rock in the middle of the road, Harold, he would draw a stepladder with his purple crayon to climb over it.'

Now I understood.

'Right then, in Dr Gordon's big house, me, I decided I was going to paint my way out of my world. Draw a better life for my people, my mother and her rough washer-woman's hands and aching back that kept her up all night.'

Julian was seven when he decided that he would become an artist, like Harold with his crayon, and draw himself out of poverty in their filthy suburb, Naledi, and out of the township of Soweto. At first he drew pictures of black faces sitting in shiny, fancy cars. A handsome father at the wheel and the children all in their finest clothes. Everyone was smiling. In another picture he even parked a car in front of a two-storied house set on rolling lawns and wrote at the top, 'This house belongs to the Mambasa family.'

'But when my mother found those pictures that I had proudly taped to our shanty wall she ripped them down, tore them into a hundred pieces and whipped me with the long, hard handle of a broom, yelling that I was never to draw such terrible things again.'

'Why was your mother so upset? I don't understand,' I said, shocked at what his mother had done to him for simply drawing.

Julian put his sketchpad down and came towards me. I was five foot six inches in stockinged feet but Julian was a towering six foot three. Dark, gleaming brow, warm, oval eyes and large, square hands that moved ever so gracefully like the wings of an eagle, stretching and reaching into the open air when he wanted to make a particular point take flight.

'Me also, Ruby, me too. I didn't understand then, but when I was done crying she rubbed a warm cloth on my stinging legs and told me that – *Hai!* – we could be arrested and put in jail for having such pictures in our home. That drawing black people like us living like white people was wrong and not allowed.'

Julian dug his hands into his paint-smeared overall pockets. He looked deeply at me before he spoke again. He smelled of old, worn leather and sweet musk.

'I never draw like that again, but, me, I keep sketching whenever I can, then painting. When my schoolteachers at Orlando West High see I have talent, they get me an old easel and some used oil paints. My mother, she was proud when I won the most-promising-artist award when I was fourteen, but she always check to make sure I am not painting anything that might get our family in trouble.'

Julian turned to look at a large charcoal drawing he had finished only a few days before that still sat on an easel.

'You are only one child, Ruby, but me, there were six of us living in two rooms, well seven really, but my father, he get home from the mines so late and leave so very early.' Julian sighed softly. 'It was like he was not even there.'

The picture was of an iron bed raised high on bricks, a single bed, but somehow Julian had managed to draw five sets of large sad eyes, attached to five long and scrawny bodies that were somehow all squeezed on to its tiny mattress, limbs across limbs, gangly feet flopping over the sides.

'Is it your . . .?'

'Yes. Me and my brothers and sisters,' he said. 'That is how we slept. But you cannot feel the cold. Hear the pipes hissing and leaking. A painting cannot give you that.' He sat down again at his easel and faced the painting, then he reached his hand out and gently traced the faces of the children in the picture.

'This is what white people want to see. Not happy black people in fancy cars.'

8

'You should be able to paint whatever you want. Surely?'

'No, it is not so. At least for now. Now I paint my people's pain. I must pretend, you see, that nothing will ever change for us.'

When Julian spoke these words it was as if he had climbed inside my very soul. Pretending was something that had become a part of me. No one at school could possibly know that I spent a great deal of time creating the appearance that I was like everyone else, that my life was normal in every way. I knew I would be shunned and an outcast if my fellow schoolmates found out that blacks were people I actually spoke to and not just when I wanted extra mashed potato or lemonade served to me. In truth, my parents were probably some of the only whites in South Africa who did not have black servants living on our property and meeting our every need. You did not have to be rich to have a black nanny who worked six days a week and late into the nights before collapsing exhausted in her small ill-lit room on the family grounds. Thirty rand a month and food bought you her loyalty. My parents did not believe in having servants. Black people sat at our dining-room table as guests and ate dinner with us while Mother and I cleared their plates away at the end of the meal.

To make certain that I appeared to be 'normal', I worked hard and got straight As. I was a school prefect and popular with loads of friends and a drawer full of ribbons from winning athletic events. But my shameful truth was that I, Ruby Winters, felt like a fraud and it was just a matter of time before I was found out.

Chapter Two

It was about two miles from the top of Westcliff Ridge to school, which was in the tree-lined suburb of Saxonwold. As with most private schools in Johannesburg, the grounds were expansive, the rugby field immaculate and the swimming pool crystal clear and skimmed daily for fallen leaves. Only the offspring of the richest and most prestigious families of the area went to Barnard High School. The golden ones, as it were, of the golden city, as Johannesburg was sometimes called. The school, formerly called Theason High, had recently been renamed in honour of the famous Cape Town heart surgeon, Christiaan Barnard, who had performed the world's first open heart transplant. It pleased me that our school was now named after someone who understood the workings of the heart.

On most days I rode my bike to school, weather permitting. My gym shoes on, my school dress tucked carefully under my legs to stop it from blowing up and embarrassing me. I would pull my long dark hair into a tight, high ponytail that I instantly took down once I'd jumped off my bike on to school property. I would wind my way down the wide avenues, taking the street's bends and curves in my stride and enjoying the quiet of 6.30 a.m., for school began at seven. These were the moments of the day I relished almost as much as my afternoon time with Julian, when my mind was opened by the crisp winds that filled my head with blissful emptiness, before maths formulas and history dates and literature quotes would claim that space from it.

In those solitary early morning hours I would ride peacefully for most of the way, but in the final minutes, as I pedalled up the last hill with my breath coming in faster and faster gasps, I felt suspended between my solitude and the noise of active life. Below me was the bustling clamour of students, now racing in grey-and-blue uniforms to make it through the prominent stone gateposts that marked the entrance into the school quadrangle.

In less than a minute I would be carried in on the wave of other student cyclists and satchel-carrying teenagers rushing to the first morning class. On some days I would backpedal furiously and hold myself still on the top of the rise for once I freewheeled down the hill I became Ruby, popular girl at school. The longing to really be known by someone would fill me with a sickening dizziness that would cause me to almost topple to the ground.

'You can't run your life only on emotions,' were my father's concerned words to me when I told him that I sometimes felt overwhelmed with the difficulty of keeping our lives at home a secret. 'To have control in our lives we have to take control of our emotions. Keep them close by, but never let them run the show.'

I tried to take his words in, tried to stop my thoughts and fears from taking over, but I was not enough like my father. I suppose that was why he could represent a murderer and an innocent abused black man all in one week. His feelings didn't impair his legal mind, didn't cause him to buckle under his personal convictions.

'Stay calm, stay clear, don't show yourself,' I told myself firmly as I lifted my foot from the brake and sailed down the hill, joining the throng.

'Hey, Ruby!'

'See you in fourth period.'

'Catch me at the tuck shop later.'

The words of my friends whizzed by me.

I smiled back.

Now I was one of them.

Chapter Three

Halfway through geography class, Desmond's hands began to stroke my hair. Smooth, even stokes that I knew were his signal to have me turn round. I never did. After a few unsuccessful minutes he would lean forward on his desk and try to get as close as he could to my ear.

'C'mon, Ruby, turn round. I wanna show you something . . .'

His breath felt warm and smelled like spicy cinnamon. Telltale wrappers of gum always filled his ink well. He reeked of good breath and old money, but not necessarily of good breeding.

Our desks were miniature oak antiques, purchased when the school was first built after World War I. We never had enough room on the desktop for our large textbooks and I often wondered if perhaps students had been smaller back then. I tried to imagine them racing through the same gates and quadrangle. I wondered too if there were annoying rich boys like Desmond Granger who thought that everyone and everything was his right to claim.

'I have something for you, Red Jewel . . .' Desmond pressed his fingers into my shoulder.

I shrugged his hand off and let out a sigh of annoyance. 'Des . . . stop!' I hissed back.

'Can someone tell me what the three main exports of Ecuador are?' Miss Radcliffe turned and faced the blackboard and wrote in big letters 'EXPORT?'.

'Rubies!' Desmond shouted out.

The class tittered and I felt my cheeks grow hot. I kicked back at Desmond's chair.

Miss Radcliffe spun round and shot Desmond and me a marble-eyed glare with her beady eyes. 'You two need to stop playing footsie and . . .'

'We're not!' I blurted out.

The class tittered again.

My best friend, Monica, rolled her eyes at me and gave me that here-we-go-again look. She tossed her long blonde mane in Desmond's direction and shook her head at him. A combination of a flirt and a scold.

Monica and I were opposites. She was light while I was dark, both in hair colour and personality. This was probably why we were drawn to each other on the first day of kindergarten. I had cried while she had smiled and blown her mother a kiss as our parents made a hasty exit from the cheerful classroom. With tearstained cheeks I had followed Monica into the sandpit where we spent the entire year playing together. We did not see each other again once we started at separate 'big schools' but found each other again on the first day of high school. We picked up where we had left off, minus the buckets and spades.

Miss Radcliffe straightened the glasses on her nose and bobbed in her crane-like fashion over to my desk. She had a long, wiry, coat-hanger-shaped frame that hunched forward, her head hanging lower than her shoulders, her long nose pointing towards the ground.

'Ruby Winters,' she tapped her long finger on my desk. 'Desmond Granger, you are both school prefects, kindly behave as such!' She turned on her spindly ankles and returned to the blackboard. 'Now then, class . . . someone . . . the main exports of Ecuador!'

I scraped my undersized chair as far forward as it would go, away from Desmond's insistent fingers. Since we were eleven years old he had been trying to get me to meet him alone, after school, for an afternoon boat ride on Zoo Lake or even an ice cream at Butterworth's Sweet Shoppe. Although Desmond was strikingly handsome and one of the most popular boys in the school, his rich-boy, overly confident air made him unattractive to me. But Desmond, who was always used to getting what he wanted, refused to give up.

It had become the betting-joke of our matric class. 'Would Des get Ruby to go on a date with him before our final school year was over?'

A note flew over my head and landed with a whoosh on my desk. I quickly grabbed it and hid it on my knees out of Miss Radcliffe's sight.

'"Cocoa and coffee." Very good, Stacey. You must have done your homework.' The chalk scraped painfully across the board as she wrote the words next to 'EXPORT?'.

I felt the hair rise like porcupine quills on the back of my neck.

I'm coming over to your house tonight. No questions asked.

Kisses

Des

PS Hey, come to think of it, does anyone ever get to come over to your house?

I crumpled the note in my fist slowly so that it wouldn't make any noise and draw attention. Without turning round I shook my head vigorously, hoping Desmond would get my fervent response.

'Uh uh,' he whispered, just loud enough for me to hear. 'I'm coming . . . over.' He snickered at his innuendo, then let out a loud snort-laugh.

'Desmond!' Miss Radcliffe squeaked, her head launching into a rat-tat-tat barrage of bobbing motion. 'What in heaven's name is the matter with you? Enough!'

Desmond stood and pulled his tall frame to its full upright position. He straightened his blue-and-maroon school tie, then raised one eyebrow and stared with penetrating green eyes at Miss Radcliffe, now almost eye-to-eye with him as she stood inches from his desk, one hand placed firmly on her non-existent hip.

'I do so apologize to you and the class –' his voice as smooth and creamy-sounding as vanilla pudding – 'but it's Ruby's fault, you see . . . she's such a distraction. And I'm just a growing boy who can't contain myself.' His hand patted his crotch.

Miss Radcliffe took a horrified leap back from him.

The class burst into a din of raucous laughter. Some of

the boys clapped and whooped as Desmond was led by a beet-red Miss Radcliffe to the principal's office.

As he was ushered past me I heard his voice through the din, 'You owe me, Ruby. All this punishment I take for you . . . Later, beauty.' He turned to me and winked as he passed by.

I looked away from his gaze and jolted my head to stare out of the window, forcing the jeers and laughter of my classmates to fade into the background. Our row of desks was closest to the large windows that faced a small side garden off the main quadrangle. I focused my eyes on a gardener in faded blue overalls as he bent to grasp the handles of a wheelbarrow that he had filled with weeds. He wore a wide-brimmed straw hat that looked like it must have once belonged to a fine lady, for there was still a cluster of wilted silk flowers in its centre. He stopped after a few seconds and pushed the feminine hat off his forehead and wiped his brow with the back of his hand, giving me a quick vision of his lined, dark face. He reached for his back and rubbed it slowly with his free hand.

The old gardener must have felt my gaze because suddenly he looked up. He shielded his eyes from the sun's rays and spotted me through the classroom window. I raised my hand ever so tentatively and waved at him just as Miss Radcliffe returned, minus Desmond, slamming the classroom door with a loud smack.

The old man lifted his wrinkled hand and waved back. Then he smiled and tipped his straw hat towards me before grasping the wheelbarrow in both hands and moving slowly across the green expanse of lawn.

I wanted to bolt from my seat and run to catch up with him. I longed to flee the screeching teacher and the tittering friends and the insistent boy who would not leave me alone.

Perhaps, once I reached him, I would ask the old man how many years he had worked as a gardener for our school and what kind of flowers were his favourite. I was certain no one had ever asked him that question or even cared to know. He was an invisible black man working in the world of affluent whites. It occurred to me how strange that was. Black was such a strong noticeable colour and white closer to transparent. Or maybe through the eyes of others, black was a dark abyss. A infinite hole of nothingness.

But, of course, I never got up the nerve to leave the classroom and catch up with him. Ruby Winters, school prefect, had to set an example. And right then Ecuador was waiting.

Chapter Four

My mother's art gallery, simply named Annabel's, was my after-school refuge when a day had been particularly hard. Here the world was defined by shapes and colours that spoke to me in a language far more meaningful than the squawking sounds that came from Miss Radcliffe. It was a place of canvassed anguish, splotches of emotion thrown on empty spaces, etched hope and joy in lightly pencilled strokes, and where, no matter how abstract some of the works were, everything made sense. Ever since I was a young child, each hushed gallery room was a haven of quiet comfort to me.

It was there that I pedalled furiously to after school that day.

'Mother!' I yelled, my voice echoing through the stark oval reception area. 'Where are you?'

'Dahling one, what's the Mommy Emergency?' Dashel, Mother's assistant, came out from behind a large oil that he was about to hang in the Gallery Grande, the largest of the seven galleries that were arranged in a circular configuration off the reception area. Everyone called him 'Dashing Dashel' because he was just that. Coiffed greying hair, neatly groomed goatee and his classic black polo neck and pressed gaberdine black trousers were his 'gallery uniform', as Mother called it.

'Lordy, but we are looking hot and bothered today, young lady.' Dashel brushed a strand of unruly hair off my face.

'Dash, it's school,' I blurted out.

'Now, now, poppet, tell Uncle D everything. Annabel is tied up with the art critic from *Die Vaderland*.' He flared his nostrils as if a bad smell had just passed under them. 'You know, the Afrikaans newspaper.'

'What do they want?' I followed him into his stark black-and-white office.

'God alone knows. Probably want a juicy story on our latest run-in with the police over Kumalo's arrest outside the gallery.' He swish-swished ahead of me and threw himself dramatically into the swivel chair behind his pristine desk and arched his neck back like a dying swan. 'I am sick, sick of the blasted police.' He ran a hand over his forehead as if there were beads of perspiration glistening there. 'Why won't they leave our poorest artists alone?'

'Father says it's because art is a more powerful weapon for change than guns.'

'Well then –' Dashel lifted his head up and looked me in the eye – 'Kumalo is the biggest goddamned cannon of them all!'

Christopher Kumalo had been Mother's most successful protégé. He had come to her gallery almost three years ago with a tattered artist's portfolio filled with extraordinary sketches of pigeons in various stages of death. Some were trapped on barbed-wire fences, their bowels exposed; others were flattened under the wheels of armed tanks, called 'hippos' because of their massive size, that rolled into the townships and brought with them uniformed men who shot at anything they chose, including children. Still others in Kumalo's pigeon sketches lay emaciated and starving in dirty gutters. These were the riches that Kumalo brought Mother, for he himself was penniless and ailing from hepatitis.

I remember the night that Mother brought Kumalo home and let him stay in our spare bedroom. She got him medical treatment from one of her politically active doctor friends, who came secretly, late at night, to check on his progress. Kumalo was already a man in his forties when, through Mother's international connections, he reached artistic fame abroad almost a year ago. His fame in South Africa began to grow, much to the government's chagrin. Kumalo lived covertly in our home and would leave our grounds under cover of night to return to Soweto to capture quick impressions of township life. He would return to our house at four or five in the morning when Mother, or sometimes I, would make him hot chocolate before he began sketching in rapid, earnest strokes the impressions and imprints from his night in Soweto. His haste to capture what he had seen, before the police got to him, made him a nervous, passionate and focused man. After his last arrest, Mother had him sent to stay with an art dealer in Cape Town, a much more accepting and liberal city, but still one where Kumalo would have to watch his back. Black fame brought with it dangerous scrutiny. His newfound fame had also put Mother's gallery under a political microscope.

'Are they still going to try him?' I plunked myself down in the cool leather chair across from Dashel's desk. The backs of my sweaty legs attached themselves like octopus tentacles to the soft, buttery upholstery.

'Your brilliant father will get him off on some legal technicality, don't worry. Now what's bothering you, sweet thing?' Dashel took a sip of mineral water from a crystal tumbler.

'Nothing . . . it's really nothing. Not compared to other things . . .' My voice trailed off.

'It was important when you came leaping in here like a frenzied impala.' He ran his finger along the rim of the glass. 'Stop being so damn perfect. There's room for only one saint in this gallery and that space is already taken by your mother.'

'It's about a boy, Uncle D.'

'Yes, I know all about boys . . .' He flashed me a pearly white-capped smile. 'Heaven knows, sometimes I wish I didn't.'

'He's handsome, smart and confident.'

'Sounds pretty dreamy to me –' Dashel raised a well-groomed eyebrow – 'and obviously rich if he goes to the same school as you.'

'I can't stand him. He won't leave me alone!' I felt the damp creases behind my knees begin to itch.

Dashel stood, sauntered round his desk and positioned

himself on the arm of my chair, carefully rearranging his trouser legs. 'Now then, is it a fever we're having or a menstrual moment, dahling one?' He touched my forehead with the back of his cool hand.

I let out a deep breath and lay back on the soft leather. 'You don't understand. No one does.' I closed my eyes and breathed in the smell of pottery lacquer and pine-scented floor cleaner. Then the subtle fragrance of perfumed mandarins filled my nostrils.

'What doesn't anyone understand?' Mother breezed in. I didn't even have to open my eyes to know that she was standing looking down earnestly at me. She touched my arm lightly and patted it a few times. Her hands were small and delicate like a Japanese porcelain doll's.

'Ruby, you look awful . . .'

'Gee thanks.' I squinted up at her.

'Thandi!' Mother called out in a sing-song voice in the direction of the gallery kitchen, 'Be a love and bring Ruby a glass of that fizzy lemonade to drink, will you?'

'Yes, I come now, madam,' Thandi's voice echoed back, her voice travelling through the uncluttered and spacious oval rooms in loud circular motions that bounced back like a boomerang.

The gallery's main staff of two had been working for Mother for many years. They were like family to me. They had watched me change and grow since the day I sat and scribbled with crayons on the gallery walls much to my mother's alarm. Dashel had called my first artistic expression a 'brilliant kindergarten-inspired mural!'.

'*Hai*, but you are looking awful, Miss Ruby!' Thandi whistled through the two vacant spaces in her mouth where her front teeth should have been.

'Thanks.' I reached up and took the drink from her. 'Mother said the same thing.'

I gulped down the fizzy soda, its coolness swirling against the back of my throat while three pairs of eyes watched with overly protective concern. I hadn't realized how thirsty I was until the last drop was gone.

'Methinks our young lady has been revived.' Dashel went to sit behind his desk with a triumphant flourish.

'*Yirra, man*, but you is looking too thin to me, Miss Ruby. God'struth!' Thandi was a big-boned Cape-coloured woman with wiry bunches of hair grouped together and tied with festive strips of cloth like haystacks. She had worn her hair that way since she first came to work for Mother almost ten years ago. Being a person of 'mixed race' was difficult enough but being a Cape coloured in Johannesburg was even worse – unless, of course, you were Thandi, and got to live in the large back room of the gallery and, in return for free board, kept the gallery immaculate. Cape coloureds were generally looked down upon by blacks and whites alike. Being of mixed blood, they belonged in neither group. They were a lost people in many ways. They often drank too much and developed their own strange jargon, a mixture of English and Afrikaans and black languages. Most of them lived in the Cape Province but Thandi had fallen in love with a Sotho dockworker, Hendriks, and had followed him to Johannesburg when he was found to have no legal papers for living in the Cape. He fled before the police could catch him with Thandi close at his heels.

'He was a *bliksem*! A *tsotsie*. A good-for-nuthin piece a nuthin!' she would cluck and hiss through the gap in her teeth if anyone ever asked her about Hendricks. 'Hell, I used up all my own bleddy cash for rides in the backs of stinky lorries to get *ons* here!' She would shake her head so vigorously that her hair-stacks would bounce against each other as if they were caught in the path of a powerful hurricane.

We all knew better than to ask her about the man who had left her, literally, in the middle of a busy intersection on their first day in the 'City of Gold'. Fortunately for Thandi that intersection happened to be right across the road from Mother's gallery.

'Ruby sweetheart.' Mother knelt beside me. 'What's the fuss all about?'

'She's in love!' Dashel exclaimed.

I jumped to my feet almost knocking Mother to the ground. 'I am so not! Dashel, I told you, I hate him!'

'Ruby, lower your voice.' Mother dusted herself off and rose to her petite five foot one inches.

'So much passion, dahling . . . a fine line between love and hate. Uncle D knows about these things.' Dashel placed a hand over his well-preserved heart.

'*Yirra*, but you are an angry one today. Like hot piri-piri sauce!' Thandi licked her finger and placed it on my cheek, then quickly pulled it away as if it had been scalded. 'Tzzz.'

'Why doesn't anyone understand?' my voice came out weak and quivering.

'Come.' Mother led me out of Dashel's office. 'Honestly, you two ought to know better.' She gave them both a withering stare. I followed her tiny light steps to her office, which was an oval pod of warmth and bright colours.

When I was comfortably settled on her oversized apricot couch I told her how miserable I was at school because of Desmond. I had planned on telling her that he had threatened to show up uninvited at our house that night but decided that she had more than enough to worry about at the moment. I would face that horrible situation when it arose.

'I know how it feels when people try to make your life miserable. Deliberately.' She said the word slowly, as if it were painful to get each syllable out of her small bow-shaped mouth. 'The journalist from *Die Vaderland* who just left was trying to get me to admit that I was wrong to let artists cross illegally into Sandton. It's such a ridiculous joke.' She ran a small hand through her wispy blonde hair. 'It's absurd that on this side of Rulin Road you are in Sandton, but on the other side of the street you're in Johannesburg.' She looked at me with her pale-blue eyes. 'I told the reporter that the police ought to have better things to do than lie in wait on the gallery side of the street to catch my artists who have legal passes that allow them in Johannesburg but not ones that allow them into Sandton.'

'That's how they got Kumalo last time, Mother. Isn't it?'

She sighed and drummed her fingers on her red lacquered desk. 'Yes. They arrested him as he crossed the street.' She smacked her hand hard on the table. 'The imbeciles. See, Ruby, there might be a fine line between love and hate, I don't know. What I do know is that there's a fine line on this very street and we are on the side of danger.'

'I'm glad you sent Kumalo to Cape Town. What about Julian?'

'Ah, Julian. I won't let him walk from the bus stop to the gallery ever. Much too risky now.' She flipped through a stack of mail that was piled on her desk. 'Now about the boy . . . whether you love him or hate him is not what matters. What matters is that you don't give him the power to ruin your day or make you not want to go to school. See, then he has won.' She tore open a large blue envelope with a pointy fingernail. 'Don't let him win, Ruby.' She tossed the empty envelope into a wicker basket and smiled up at me. 'You are, after all, my daughter and nobody gets the better of us Winters girls. Not prying journalists or snotty, spoiled boys.' She gave me a long-lashed wink.

Chapter Five

There are certain moments in my life that I can stop and look back and say, Ah yes. It was that very day, that very situation, those very moments when everything took a turn in a certain direction, and my life, and that of my family, would be forever altered. That night became such a moment. Everything that happened thereafter would lead us on a path that we had not expected. I have often wondered that perhaps, had I known how important that night would be, would I have wanted anything to be different? Was there something anyone could have said or done that would have changed the eventual outcome? My answer has always been an unequivocal, No.

Two things occurred, both announced by a loud knock on our large oak front door. The first was less of a knock and more of a savage scratching, like a chicken scraping its sharp claws on the hard surface. It was my mother who rose from the dining-room table leaving my father and me with half-eaten plates of cottage pie and gem squash. The time was eight o'clock and I could hear the deep, low sound of the grandfather clock in the foyer marking the hour as Father stood suddenly, pushing his plate back and dropping his white linen napkin on the freshly starched tablecloth.

'Annabel, wait!' He strode from the room after her. 'Let me get it . . . how in heavens did someone get past the gates . . .?'

It was on the eighth deep chime from the melancholy clock that I heard the door open and Mother's voice, a shrill, anguished wail, filled the house together with the last sad chime. Eight. It said eight.

'Julian, my God!' she screamed. 'What have they done to you?!'

On hearing his name I sprang from my seat and raced to the front door. Mother was leaning over Julian who lay face down, hands splayed out in front of him across the threshold of the front door. Father was wrenching his red-and-gold tie from his neck and in one fast movement he bound it tightly round Julian's bicep. A rivulet of blood ran boldly across his slashed fingers. There were deep gashes in his arms and each finger bore a purple-etched wound.

Father unbuckled his belt, swiftly removed it, then bound it tightly round Julian's other leaking arm.

Ruby. It is your name. It is also the colour that we bleed. I heard Julian's voice echo inside my head, remembering the words he had once said while I watched him paint a crimson sun over Soweto's slums on a taut canvas.

Blood. My name means blood, I thought as I twisted my table napkin tightly.

Mother cradled Julian's face in her hands as Father

rolled him slowly over and slid him gently forward on to the smooth, polished entrance-hall floor, slamming the door shut and locking every bolt. I watched Father's large fingers, stained red, and felt a rush of love for him. He would protect us all. Father would keep us safe.

Julian moaned and tried to lift his head. I moved, as if in slow motion, to him. This was not happening, could not be happening. My eyes clouded as I wiped droplets off his cheeks, his eyes, his cracked, bloodied lips. The world was suddenly unclear as I looked down at him through a misty veil.

'Who did this to you?' Father whispered close into his ear. 'Who, Julian, tell us . . . who?'

It was not until ten days later and one hundred and forty-seven stitches that had been needed to sew up the damage to his young body that Julian was able to let the word spill from his swollen mouth: '*Tsotsies.*'

Thugs. No one in particular. Just a band of roving young men with hunger in their bellies and hatred in their hearts from years of living the raw, hard life in a township. They turned their rage on one of their own. The *tsotsies* had perhaps taken note of Julian's better clothes, his clean shirt and upright walk. They had perhaps watched from across the potholed dusty street as he sketched a woman carrying a large water pail on top of her head, a baby tied to her ample back. They knew what would hurt him most, what part of his being was sacred to him. His fine artist's hands. Later he told me how the *tsotsies* held him down and sliced each finger, making sure to cut deeper into the right than the left. They had watched which hand needed to suffer the most damage, which wrist flicked deftly back and forth in charcoaled strokes. They wanted to ensure that Julian would never wear a clean shirt again. Never capture an image on paper again. What they did not know was that Julian carried a secret weapon they had lost long ago. Passion was what kept him moving forward, kept him waking each morning and catching two buses to our house so that he could share his passion with the outside world. And his pain. A yearning for something better for himself, for all of his people. Passion is what brought him broken and bleeding back to our house that night. It would be more than a month before he could hold a piece of charcoal in his scarred fingers again, but when he finally did his work radiated a luminous pain that spun itself tightly round your heart. For the images that left his aching fingers were harsher and more hauntingly real. The *tsotsies* could tear at his limbs with their switchblades but they could not shear into his soul, and Julian's passion seemed now to burn even more brightly.

After that night Julian moved in permanently with us. Safe behind our substantial gates, where thugs could not cut away jealous pieces of him.

The second knock at the door came right after Mother had taken Dr Jacobs upstairs to tend to Julian. Dr Jacobs, a portly, bald-headed man who had been our family doctor since I was a young child, was bounding up the stairs, stethoscope swinging wildly, black doctor's bag slapping against his stout legs within twenty minutes of

Mother's insistent call. 'Not Baragwanath, he's not putting foot in Soweto ever again . . . Get here now! He's damn near bleeding to death!' Mother had slammed the phone down.

I was about to go up the stairs after Mother but a loud bold knock on our front door caught me off guard mid-stair-flight. 'Don't let anybody in!' Mother raced up the stairs after Dr Jacobs and shouted down at me without turning, 'Especially if it's the police . . . Ruby! Oh God . . .'

I felt slippery and slow, turning, as I did, on unsteady legs that carried me somehow to the front door.

'Who is it?' came out of me in an unnaturally high-pitched tone.

'It's the man of your dreams . . .' the voice through the door answered.

I didn't recognize it through the heavy oak-panelled door and asked again who it was.

'Oh, Ruby . . . I told you I would be here tonight. A certain little note from me to you . . .'

'Desmond. No!' I said softly, and leaned an icy cheek against the door. 'Please no,' I whispered to myself. 'Not now, please not tonight.'

Desmond rapped loudly on the door again. 'C'mon, it's impolite not to let a guest in . . . especially one that you're expecting,' he chuckled. 'Don't be rude, Ruby,' he laughed. He banged loudly and raised his voice, 'RUDE RUBY!'

I looked down at the remains of smeared blood that covered the foyer floor and quickly unbolted all the locks and opened the front door just enough to squeeze myself through to the outside flagstone patio, then shut the door tightly behind me.

An overpoweringly strong smell of musk and pine filled my nostrils. Desmond was dressed in neatly pressed khaki trousers and a royal-blue cashmere sweater. He looked perfect, undamaged; he wore his wealth well and had probably come straight from dinner at the Country Club, where his family had donated funds for an indoor swimming pool. Desmond was the fastest backstroke swimmer in our school.

He grinned down at me from his superior height. 'Wow, you look . . .'

I watched his eyes travel down my unkempt blood-stained shirt, then up to my dishevelled hair. I placed my hands over the near browning stain on my shirt breast pocket.

'Desmond, there was an accident here tonight . . . I can't let you . . .'

'What kind of accident?' Desmond cocked his head and held me in his green-eyed gaze.

'A bad one.' I looked away. 'Someone got hurt.'

'Someone like who?' he asked with piqued curiosity. 'A family member, a servant?'

'A servant,' I blurted out. 'The gardener.' I flashed back to the old gardener at school, wiping sweat from his brow. 'He cut himself quite badly on some shears . . . there's blood . . .'

'Better put him on a bus to Baragwanath. He can't get treatment at *our* hospitals.'

'It's taken care of,' I said sharply.

'Well then, what's the problem?' He moved closer and touched my hair. 'Mmm, I think I like you a little messy. Let me in, wild thing.' He leaned forward and brushed his lips against my hair.

I took a step back and felt the doorknob jab into my back as I pushed Desmond away.

'How did you get through the gates? You really need to leave!'

'Temper, temper.' He grinned. 'Hot and bothered is such a good look for you.' He encircled the back of my neck with his hand. 'You will kiss me one day, you know . . .' I pursed my lips together tight. 'Yes, one day, Ruby . . . you will beg me to kiss you, but until then I'm going to have to partake without your permission.' He pressed his body hard against mine and forced his tongue into my unyielding mouth as the doorknob jabbed fiercely into my spine. I heard Father's voice calling my name from inside – 'Ruby! Where are you?' – as I clamped my teeth down hard on Desmond's tongue. He let out a yelp and staggered backwards, covering his mouth. He looked down, disbelieving, into his hands where fresh blood had fallen.

'I'm here, Father! Outside,' I yelled back. 'It's okay, I'm okay!' I shouted as I held on tightly to the sides of the front door for support.

Desmond took a deliberate step towards me. His grinning confidence was replaced with an alarming sneer.

'So . . .' He wiped his blood-soaked finger across my mouth. 'That's how you –' he made a deliberate circle around my mouth – 'like it.' Then he dragged his hand across my shirt making sure that he cupped my left breast harshly as his hand smeared a bloody trail down my shirt.

'Bitch!' Desmond spat a mouthful of injured spittle at my feet. He turned on his heels and walked towards the gates that hung wide open. Julian must have somehow managed not to lose his keys in the ambush, but in leaving the gates open he had allowed Desmond easy access to our home.

Father was standing in the entrance hall as I slipped quickly back into the house. There was a mangled look of love and relief and bewilderment on his face as he saw me. 'Ruby!' He clutched me to him as I ran into his outstretched arms, his voice cracking as he held me close.

Chapter Six

How could it be that at a time when people were being mistreated, when children went hungry and families were divided and did not see each other for months on end and children in Soweto didn't have enough pencils to hold in their stark classrooms, that we played hockey and won horse-jumping trophies and competed in swimming galas and sipped lemonade and ate homemade cookies at half-time during netball matches?

Surely I could not have been the only one in the school cafeteria who noticed the bowed head of the young black girl, who must have been of school-going age, serving us steaming plates of hot bangers and mash. Did no other student notice the look of longing on her face as she took a furtive glance over at our glossy textbooks while she cleared away the plates? If there were such a student, he or she did not reveal themselves. Everyone seemed lost in the latest plans for the upcoming school dance as they shovelled food into their mouths without giving the young girl even a perfunctory nod of thanks.

'C'mon, Ruby, you've got to co-chair the Disco Ball,' my friend Clive urged.

'Yeah, you and Desmond should co-chair and then it would be called "The Disco Brawl"!' someone down the long cafeteria table yelled out.

Desmond had returned to school after our bloody encounter and had made it clear to everyone that I was the number-one she-witch of the matric class and anyone who spoke to me would no longer be a friend of his. To my surprise, our classmates were fairly evenly divided, with many of the boys, long since jealous of all the attention Desmond got from the girls, happily siding with me, together with a handful of girls who Desmond had snubbed or ignored at one time or another. But the most hurtful act of all was my very best friend, Monica, who had tossed her long blonde mane and marched off to Desmond's camp. I suppose I should have sensed that she had a crush on him because every time I'd mentioned how despicable Desmond was Monica had always found a way to defend him. Desmond knew how close we were and that the loss of my best friend would be a huge blow to me. In his calculated and manipulative way he had turned his magic charm on her and she was, it appeared, now under his spell. Monica, who never scratched too far below the surface and always took people at face value, was clearly totally oblivious to the fact that she was just a convenient weapon in Desmond's war against me. From what I could see from across the cafeteria, they were now something of an 'item', with her spoon-feeding gobs of soft mashed potato into his not yet fully healed mouth.

I felt a jolt of hollow pain. I had lost my best friend and had more enemies than friends at school now.

Scrutiny of my life and the life of my family was the last thing I needed. We now had a black man living the life of a white man in our home. He dined with us, sat on the same upholstered chairs, ate off the same fine china plates and slept in a bed with the softest of sheets that were made of one hundred per cent Egyptian cotton in a room that was just down the hall from my very own.

'No one must know, Ruby.' Mother and Father had sat me down the day after Julian's bloody attack. 'Our lives might be in danger,' Father said gruffly.

'We aren't trying to scare you, darling,' Mother had added, 'it's just that we don't want to draw attention . . . you understand?' She brushed a strand of hair off my face. 'If anyone finds out . . .'

'I would never do anything to hurt us. Or Julian.' My eyes moved back and forth between them. They both looked tired and drawn. 'I promise.'

I guarded the secrecy of Julian fiercely, not just for my parents' sake, but for my own. For me, having been an only child my whole life, he was like a wonderful older brother. I could share pieces of myself with him that I would not dare share with anyone else.

'What does love feel like?' I asked Julian as I knelt beside his bed and wrapped rolls of white bandages round his wounds.

Julian chuckled. 'It feels like a very bad stomach ache that only goes away when you are near the person who has your heart.'

'It should be your heart that hurts then, not your stomach.'

'Ah, that comes later.' Julian winced as he tried to prop himself up on his freshly bandaged hands.

'When is that?'

'When it is all over.' He smoothed the bed sheets down clumsily with his white club-like appendages. 'It is then that the heart hurts.'

'There should be thick bandages to wrap round a heart to help it heal faster,' I said.

'There are, Ruby.'

'What are they?'

'The gauze of time.' His eyes suddenly must have felt heavy for he closed them slowly as he spoke. 'I am rambling . . . all this pain medication that Dr Jacobs makes me take. It makes me speak mumbo-jumbo like a crazy man.'

'That's not crazy talk. It's beautiful,' I said. 'And sad too.'

'You think?' His eyes gradually opened. 'Yes, beauty and pain are close companions.' Julian smiled weakly and lifted his bandaged hand and pointed it in my direction. 'Beauty . . .' he said, then turned his hand towards his own chest, 'and pain.'

'I am not beautiful.' I blushed deeply.

'Yes, you are. And one day someone will look into your eyes and tell you just how beautiful you are inside and out. And you will believe it when you are ready to know that it is true.'

Chapter Seven

Rugby has never been a sport for the faint at heart. Here men and boys pit themselves against each other flesh to flesh. Muscle to muscle. Might to might. Protective clothing and gear is left for sissy sports. Shorts, rugby boots and striped rugby shirts is their simple uniform. Headgear is worn only by the locks whose ears get mashed between the thighs of other men in the sweaty scrum. It prevents them from getting 'cauliflower ears'. Elbow guards, knee pads and groin cups are never used. Jock straps, however, are a must.

While my father detested rugby for its boorish brutality, most men considered it the king of all South African sports. A national sport that was played by 'real men' and boys who were on their way to becoming 'real men'. Fifteen 'tough okes' per team kicked and pushed and charged each other for possession of a tear-shaped pigskin ball that had to be passed backwards to a player before it was punted high in the air through tarnished goal posts. Bloody noses, bruises and broken bones were common-place. I saw it as a modern-day pastime speckled with flashes of bygone gladiators in the arena and damsels clutching at their breasts from the sidelines as their brave men fell.

It was compulsory for everyone in our school to attend every rugby match whether you wanted to or not. Roll call was taken as we filed on to the foreign or familiar home rugby field by school prefects. Since I was a prefect I dared not miss a single match.

Our school's rugby team was one of the best amongst the English-speaking high schools. They wore our school colours, maroon and gold, proudly. Regal and gleaming, our handpicked brawny lads made Barnard High a force to be reckoned with and to fear on the field. Of course, Desmond was one of the chosen fifteen and played the important position of scrum-half. We usually competed against other English schools like King Edwards, Marist Brothers and Parktown High, and generally won, but it was rare for our team to be pitted against the Afrikaans-speaking high schools whose teams were known to be formidable.

As much as there was forced separation between blacks and whites there was almost as great a separation between the English and Afrikaans-speaking whites of our country, but that division was self-imposed by both groups. Longstanding enemies since the Anglo-Boer War of almost eighty years earlier, the descendants of Holland and the descendants of England still stood their colonial ground on opposite sides of a land already divided.

'Waste of a Friday afternoon as far as I'm concerned,' Father grumbled as he drove me through the unfamiliar neighbourhood of Newberry Park, glancing down occasionally at the printed school flyer that had directions to the well-known private Afrikaans high school, Steunmekaar.

'It's school policy, especially since I'm a prefect.' I fiddled with the elephant-hair bracelet that Thandi had given me on my most recent visit to the gallery.

'Steunmekaar . . . Support each other, that's what it means,' Father said as he pulled through the large brick gateposts that marked the entrance to the school. 'And they do only help each other.' He swerved the car to a halt at the entrance to the gymnasium where our school was to meet before the game began.

'There have to be some Afrikaners that aren't like that,' I said, grabbing my satchel from the back seat of his spit-polished Citroën.

'Let me know when you meet one, Ruby.' Father kissed me on the cheek as I leaned through the driver's window and I could not help but notice a grim tightness in his voice as I pinned my prefect's badge on to the V-neck maroon sweater that I wore over my blue school pinafore. The afternoon was warm for a winter's day and I was glad that I had left my heavy jacket at home.

It was strange to hear Afrikaans spoken all around me. Although I had learned it as a second language since I had first started school I had never heard it spoken by so many people at once. While I was getting an A in Afrikaans the conversations around me, as I made my way into the rugby stands, were faster paced and more guttural sounding, so I could only grasp every second word or so.

'*Gister het ek in a groot veg met my ma gekry.*'

'*Werklik! Dit is nie so goed nie!*'

'*Wag vir my – ek moet my boeke in die klaskamer sit!*'

'*Maak gou!*'

'*En my pa was nie tuis nie.*'

'*Het julle die lekker meisies van Barnard gesien? Yirra, mooi, man!*'

What I managed to pick up from all the chatter was that someone had had an argument with their mother, another student wanted her friends to wait up while she put her books away and a group of Steunmekaar boys were commenting that we girls from Barnard High were pretty!

The students from Steunmekaar High did not look all that different from us. Good haircuts and straight white teeth. A few more blond crew cuts on the boys and a few more tightly woven braids on the girls, but mostly they were our counterparts. Well-to-do kids from well-to-do families.

Some of them bore the markings of their Dutch descendants: rosy, rugged cheeks and upturned noses. A handsome collection of Afrikaans blue blood that bore the names of Van Niekerk and Van Rensburg proudly.

As I took my seat in the stands I could see the back of the captain of their team, in his black shorts and black-and-red striped jersey, making his way across the field to Desmond, our team captain – a natural selection since it was usually the scrum-half who led the team. I could not help but wonder if their captain was as arrogant and stuck up as Desmond.

'Boy is he cute, even if he is Afrikaans.' Janice Harris nudged me with her plump arm as we sat side by side in

43

the stands. She was one of the less attractive girls that Desmond had snubbed and was fast becoming my new companion since the battle lines had been drawn and Monica had deserted me.

'I couldn't tell.' I tried to sound nonchalant.

'I passed him in the hallway on my way to the bathroom when we got here.' Janice riffled the one-page flyer that listed the players of both teams. 'I almost choked on my caramel. He's got the bluest eyes!' She held the piece of paper towards me and pointed a chubby finger at a place on the page. 'Johann Duikster!' She smacked her lips together when she said his name, as if it were a morsel of something sweet and delicious.

I got my first real glimpse of Johann Duikster as he shook hands with Desmond on the sidelines and nodded his head in the direction of the referee with a signal to toss the coin to decide which team would choose sides first.

He was tall with blond hair that fell haphazardly over his eyes, an aquiline nose set over a full mouth, a prominent jaw that gave him the characteristic of self-assurance.

In the next moments I don't remember if the filled-to-capacity crowd applauded enthusiastically as both teams ran on to the field or if school war cries were uttered enthusiastically from the lips of both sides. What I do remember was that my stomach lurched on a sudden roller coaster that did not stop until Johann turned away from my direction and gave his teammates a thumbs-up to say they had won the toss.

Was the game close? Were there any bloody noses or broken bones? Did the afternoon weather warm up or cool down? I don't know. I kept my eyes fixed on the one object that had taken over all my senses, that made the world around him blur and fade. Nothing in my life had prepared me for this moment, this firing up in my belly, the molten glow racing through my veins.

Johann and I never met that afternoon. Our team lost to Steunmekaar 14–13 in an emotionally charged and exciting match. As both teams filed off the rugby field with the war cry of Steunmekaar Hoër filling the early evening sky I caught one last glimpse of him, the orange-and-gold light of dusk bouncing off his fair head as he was surrounded by his teammates who smothered him in a massive bear hug. I was rather glad that his team had won. I was secretly overjoyed that Desmond had not matched up to Johann and that he and his brute-strong team had deflated our very inflated scrum-half. Desmond had shaken hands with the Steunmekaar team with flushed cheeks and an achingly forced smile across his sweaty face. He must have had his father's driver and Rolls-Royce waiting for him and made a hasty getaway, for he was nowhere to be seen as we all stood around outside talking about what a close game it had been and how Steunmekaar just got lucky that day.

Father, who was supposed to fetch me at six o'clock, was running late and I was one of the last Barnard High students left outside the unfamiliar school gates. It was growing dark as I waited patiently for Father's Citroën to come screeching into the car park with the apologetic excuse that he was stuck at a legal counsel meeting longer than expected.

'Excuse me . . .'

I snapped my head round in the direction of the voice. It belonged to a Steunmekaar girl who was standing right beside me. I had not noticed her coming up to me in the fading light.

'Forgive my English, *mejevrou*, I mean, miss, but I'm only a C student in *Engels* . . . I mean English.'

'That's okay.' I smiled back at her.

She was tall with a pixie-like blonde bob that might have looked better on a more petite girl, but her eyes were a warm brown and gave her a kind and open face.

'*My naam* is Loretta.' She held a slim hand out to me. I took it and held it in mine for a second.

'*Ruby is my naam. Aangename kennis.*' I used the formal term for 'pleasure to meet you' since we were strangers and that is what Mejevrou Brand had taught us in form one. When you greeted a friend there was a more casual salutation but I had forgotten what it was.

'*Aangename kennis, ook.*' She put her satchel on the ground between us.

'My father is late,' I said.

'*Myne ook.* I mean, mine too.'

'And it's almost dark,' I said, looking around the dimly lit quadrangle and realizing that we were now completely alone.

'It is okay,' Loretta said, sensing my sudden uneasiness, '*Moenie* worry *nie*.' She patted the wall behind her and hoisted herself up. '*Kom sit.* I will not leave you.'

46

I felt a sudden tightness in my throat as I pulled myself up on the wall beside her. Monica had left me. All those birthday cards that were signed 'Best friend forever'. All those weekend sleepovers and midnight kitchen raids. All those marathon maths test study sessions and Saturday shopping trips. Was it that easy for a boy to come along and wipe it all away?

'You are thinking a lot.' Loretta touched her temple. 'Lots of thoughts, yes?'

'Sorry.' I stammered. The air was growing colder and I shivered under my now insufficient layers of clothing.

''n Jas? You want a jacket?' Loretta asked.

'Please.'

She jumped down and unzipped her satchel to pull out a neatly folded black school blazer with the Steunmekaar emblem stitched boldly in red across its right breast pocket. She held it up to me and I took it appreciatively.

I slipped on the blazer and we sat there in the darkness, two schoolgirls waiting for our respective lifts. It occurred to me that to anyone passing by in the chilled night air we appeared to be two Afrikaans teenage girls who attended the same school and spoke the same language at home. It seemed suddenly incredible to me that, just by changing school colours, I became someone else. A chameleon of a kind. I now wore a new skin that would make people look at me in a different way – I was now a Steunmekaar girl in a uniform that got me accepted in their community. And I wondered how I would be treated if I went home with Loretta in my maroon-and-gold English school attire? Was it our colours that opened and closed doors to us?

'Ruby,' Loretta asked shyly, 'what is your school like?'

'Like yours, mostly. Except maroon and gold.'

She looked at me quizzically. 'Oh, not so different, *ja*?'

'No. Not so different at all.'

Loretta waited with me until Father's headlights caught us both in their high beam. He watched as I jumped off the wall, handed Loretta back her school blazer and hugged her goodbye. I had offered to wait with her but she said her father was always late and it was no problem for her to be alone. She was accustomed to it. We had switched back and forth between English and Afrikaans in the half hour or so that we were together, and in the end we altered our sentences into a melding of both languages. Our conversation flowed smoothly once we had fallen into a blending together of both.

Loretta and I exchanged phone numbers and when I told her how far apart we lived, she smiled her warm open smile and said simply, *''n Boer maak 'n plan.'*

I wasn't sure exactly what that meant and wondered as I pulled myself into Father's warm car and waved a quick goodbye when we passed her. She was still sitting, long legs dangling over the wall. I wanted to tell Father how Loretta offered me her jacket and how interested she was in my life. I wanted him to know that not all Afrikaners were only interested in helping each other, but the words tumbled out of me in one exuberant breath.

'I have met one.'

Chapter Eight

Julian held a paintbrush in his hands for the first time almost exactly a month after the *tsotsie* ambush. He had talked longingly to me about the sweet, tangy beer that they served at the local *shebeen* that he frequented in Soweto and told Father that he preferred the taste to the Lion lager that Father served him in large frothy ice-cold mugs. With Julian unable to do much, the two of them sat and chatted in Father's study in the late afternoons when Father returned from his office. I would sometimes slip quietly into Father's cool Persian-rugged office and listen quietly while the two men spoke. Their conversation always varied and I frequently left the quiet of the room having learned something new from one or both of them. One particular conversation disturbed me and stayed for a long while afterwards.

It began rather simply:

'How was your day, sir?' Julian enquired. He insisted on calling Father 'sir' no matter how many times Father pleaded with him to call him by his first name.

'David.' Father threw his legs up on his desk and leaned back on his plush chair, clasping his hands behind his head. 'My day was . . . long. And frustrating.'

'And why was that, sir?' Julian took a long draught of beer as I positioned myself on the arm of his chair.

'I am like a small pike battling to swim upstream in very rough and treacherous waters filled with many sharks.' Father sighed.

'The Special Branch, yes?' Julian wiped away the foam that had settled above his upper lip with the back of his hand.

'They have spies everywhere, terrified Soweto dwellers who are threatened with their lives unless they give them information.' Father ran his fingers through his tousled hair. 'They just arrested one of the best in the underground. Malufa.'

'I have heard of him.' Julian set his mug down carefully on a yellow-wood antique table beside him.

'Damn shame. A tip from a scared-stiff neighbour of his, who was told she would lose her children and her job if she didn't tell them what went on until the early hours of the morning in his shack.' Father sighed again and rubbed the crease between his brows. 'He was being groomed to be a leader for change.'

'We are not ready for change,' Julian said quietly.

'Not ready? That's absurd!' Father swung his legs off the table and leaned forward on his chair. 'Your art, Julian, your art is all about your people's dismal reality. It cries out for change. I don't understand . . .'

'Yes, my art is a plea, a cry to my people. A mirror, so that they may hold the canvas up against themselves and see the ugly face of truth. Maybe then they will say, "*Hai wena!* This is how cracked our mirror is. This is how hopeless our lives are. We must stand together and fight as one.'" Julian stood and paced the room. 'Instead, they stab the hand that shows the truth. No, sir. Until we can unite brother to brother, until we can snuff out the burning jealousy that destroys when one of us rises from the filthy ashes –' Julian ran his hand slowly along the jagged scar that ran the length of his forearm – 'then, sir, we will be ready for change.' His voice quivered as he spoke.

I looked from Julian to Father, waiting for Father to come back with one of his quick-minded answers. Something that would make perfect sense and that held infinite value and wisdom. But he sat quietly and looked deep into Julian's dark eyes, which held turbulent waters and desperate pikes in their murky orbs.

'I am so sorry,' was all he said.

'As am I, sir.'

That conversation between Father and Julian hung like a swinging chandelier in my topsy-turvy brain between terrified thoughts of the upcoming Disco Ball and my part as an accomplice to Mother's latest scheme. She was planning to have an important gallery exhibition introducing Julian and debuting his work to her affluent crowd of art influencers. She was reluctant to tell Julian the good news for fear that it would somehow short-circuit his creativity. This had happened with some of her other artists in the past, both black and white. Once she had set a date for an exhibition, their work suffered. Performance anxiety was what she called it. There would be a right moment to tell Julian, but it was not yet.

'It will upset his flow and concentration if he thinks he's painting for an audience,' she told me as we walked through her gallery, discussing which paintings would hang on which walls. I was barely able to focus on the complex task. There were twenty-five works of art to be hung and I was lost in rugby-match thoughts and Disco Ball fretting.

It had been two weeks since the Steunmekaar–Barnard game and I was surprised that images of Johann, a boy I did not know and would probably never see again, kept popping into my head, sending a tingling sensation from my pink-tinged toenails to the crown of my long dark hair.

'Is love inherently tragic, Mother?' I asked as she measured a space on one of the gallery walls in her graceful and delicate way.

'"Is love inherently tragic?" Is that a title for one of Julian's works or is that a question for me?' She gave me one of her small bow-shaped smiles.

'It's the topic of an essay that's due in English literature class next week. We have to either prove or disprove the theory using Shakespeare's works.' I held up the other end of the measuring tape for her and raised my eyes to meet hers.

'Ah, I see . . . a theoretical question . . . twenty-three inches by twelve. Write that down, Ruby.' She ran a hand along a coiled strand of coloured Ndebele beads that clung to her slender, pale neck. 'Love is neither all heart-break nor all joy. It is what we bring to it that shapes it. Sometimes the end result is a misshapen Picasso and sometimes it takes the form of a starry-night Van Gogh masterpiece, all blue and gold swirling colours that hold us eternally in its majesty and power.'

'Van Gogh maimed himself, Mother, and died in misery,' I said as I wrote down the measurements on a pad of paper.

Mother dragged an oval-shaped chair close to the wall and, lifting the hem of her purple silk skirt, she climbed gracefully on to it. She ran the tape measure from her position and I caught it and dragged it to the marked spot.

'Practical. How did I ever raise such a practical daughter?' she chuckled to the empty wall. She reeled in the tape measure with a quick zipping motion and floated off the chair. 'Ah yes, the poor wretched artist died but it is the art that lives on forever. Love can do that too.' She sashayed ahead of me into the next gallery. 'Come along, Ruby darling, this is going to be an extraordinary exhibition!'

As I followed her aimlessly, I knew which side of the argument I would take and which Shakespearian work I would use to prove my cheerless belief. It would of course be *Romeo and Juliet*. I calmed myself with the knowledge that even if Johann Duikster and I were somehow to meet we were from opposite sides of the camp. A Capulet and a Montague. An Afrikaner and an Englishman. Shakespeare knew best.

Chapter Nine

Shopping was not something I enjoyed quite as much as some of the other girls at school. When we were still best of friends, Monica had to practically drag me to the boutiques in Rosebank or Hillbrow to buy new clothes. It wasn't that I didn't like the latest styles, the embroidered gypsy cheesecloth tops, the ever-so-high platform shoes and flared bell-bottom jeans, it was that I felt that my muscular athletic legs filled out the trousers too much and looked bulky in a miniskirt. Monica used to laugh and tell me that I had a really good figure, but it was easy for her to say, with her tong-flicked Farrah Fawcett blonde hair and long, lean legs that looked fantastic in hot pants, something I would never dare to wear.

We used to make a day of it. Saturday morning shopping, lunch and sometimes an afternoon film. If we were in suburban Rosebank, we would eat at the Branded Steer where the hamburgers were juicy and delicious and the chips, drenched in tomato sauce, melted in your mouth. But, if we were in fashionable Hillbrow, where dark safety-pinned punk-rock clothing and strong-smelling woolly Afghan coats hung side by side in small, psychedelically painted stores, we would eat at Cabbages and Kings, a new vegetarian restaurant that was fast becoming popular. I liked the lentil pie while Monica ate the tofu and rice concoction, but she insisted that we stop at the cafe on the corner to buy a Crunchie bar or Peppermint Crisp afterwards.

'Too healthy!' she would laugh, her pink-painted mouth spewing chocolate in all directions.

I missed her. Missed having a best friend who enjoyed being with me no matter what we were doing. She was like cotton candy, all light and fluffy, unlike my thick-as-malt texture. We were a perfect odd coupling. Monica never asked questions about my parents or why they didn't like kids to come over after school. She was the youngest in her family, with two older brothers who doted on her and gave her beer whenever she asked, which was every weekend. They would mix it with Seven Up for her to make a beer shandy, which was, according to them, what ladies drank. Monica liked to dance and even owned a pair of neon-blue spandex leggings that she would disco dance in all around their large rambling house.

Now I had lost her to Desmond without even an argument or discussion. She had simply walked away from me when he'd decided he wanted her. I imagined that he made her choose sides. Him or me. Best friend or new boyfriend. She chose him. It hurt a lot.

It hurt even more as I walked with Janice through Hillbrow and stopped in the same stores that Monica and I used to go to. We were browsing through the racks of Spiros, one of our favourite boutiques.

'You'll look great in this, Ruby!' Janice held a lime-green halter-neck jumpsuit out to me enthusiastically.

'It's a bit flashy.' I coughed, trying to unstick the lump in my throat.

'You've got to go a bit over the top for the Disco Ball – everyone does!'

It was true. This was the one night when everyone shed their conservative school uniforms and we were allowed to wear whatever we liked. Outrageous had become the antidote for all those pent-up days in school uniform. It was the night when Barnard High's teachers turned a blind eye to the girls' micro miniskirts that barely covered anything or the boys' white shirts that were open almost to their navels and glowed neon white under the ultraviolet lights that were mounted on the walls of the auditorium.

'Ruby, c'mon, give it a whirl!' Janice pushed the jumpsuit into my hands.

'Okay, I'll try it on.' I reluctantly headed into the dressing room.

As I stripped down to my bra and pants I tried to stop the ball of disappointment from welling up and spilling over in a flood of injured tears. I would get over this, like I did everything else. I would hide how I really felt. Only Julian had seen small cracks in my less-than-perfect self.

'Well, how does it look?' Janice was practically panting outside the closed curtains.

I stepped into the lightweight spandex jumpsuit and tied the halter top behind my neck.

'It looks good,' I answered honestly. The jumpsuit was

surprisingly flattering and followed the lines of my body closely before flaring out into large bellbottoms. The bright colour offset my dark eyes and dark hair.

'Jeez, Louise!' Janice flung the curtains open before I could protest. 'You look fab!'

I blushed. 'Thanks, Janice, you're a real pal.'

It was true, she was a real pal, but not a best friend. And that would just have to do for now. Maybe just a pal was enough. If a pal decided to leave the friendship, it wouldn't hurt as much. While I paid for the jumpsuit and Janice fumbled for crumpled rand notes in her over-sized crochet purse for the flowing gypsy skirt with embroidered hemline and bell-sleeved Indian-print top, I made a silent pact that I was done with best friends for good. We ended the afternoon at Cabbages and Kings. I decided that it was high time I ordered something different, so I chose the rice and tofu concoction that was Monica's favourite. It was tasty and delicious but every mouthful burned my insides as it went down.

Janice's mother picked us up in her grey estate, swerving to an untidy halt on the corner of Piet Retief Avenue and Bishops Boulevard. She waved her wobbly arm frantically at us in case we couldn't see her. She was hard to miss with her outdated blonde beehive hairdo and flapping false eyelashes. Janice's eight-year-old brother, Gerald, was slumped down in the back of the car. His oversized body spilled over both seats and he seemed less than thrilled that he had to share the back seat with anyone.

I squeezed myself into the tiny space beside him while Janice sat next to her mother. The car smelled like day-old pizza. Mrs Harris shot a barrage of questions at me that began the second the car door was closed, while Gerald shot bits of chewed-up paper through a straw at anything he could. I was, of course, his nearest target. Janice was busy pulling her new purchases out of the bag to admire and Mrs Harris was so intent on getting as much information out of me as she could in the fifteen-minute car ride to my house that neither noticed I was being assailed by chewed-up wads of paper. I tried to block them before they hit me but it was a losing battle. For an overweight eight-year-old he had the chewing-spitting speed of a sleek cheetah.

'So, Ruby, Janice tells me that you and Monica Benson are on the outs. I never liked that girl, a flirt in a skirt, is what she is. I was at high school with her mother, you know – Lynette, she was always such a high and mighty one.' She scratched way down into the top of her coiffed hair with a long silver-painted nail that disappeared into her dyed yellow nest.

Before I had a chance to tell her that Monica's mother's name was Claudia, not Lynette, and that she grew up in Cape Town, I got shot in the ear by another gobbed-up ball of paper.

While I tried to unplug the soggy intruder, Mrs Harris's next question came at me through muffled tones.

'I hear your mother's gallery is under criminal investigation for helping communist artists. Gossip! Just nasty gossip . . .'

'Mom, you're not looking!' Janice made the gypsy skirt dance in front of her. 'Do you like it? Do you . . .?'

'I need the toilet!' Gerald whined. 'I ate too much lunch.'

I tried to think of something quick and clever to say in response to her question. Or perhaps something stupid and naive would be better, whichever came first. But instead I settled for the truth.

'My mother handles artists and their art. Not politicians and their politics, Mrs Harris,' I answered firmly but politely. I could tell that my response sailed clear over her high beehive and out of the wet-balled window. She seemed suddenly at a loss for words and turned her attention to Janice's gypsy skirt, oohing and aaahing over it in her nasal voice, then turned to Gerald, promising that they would stop at the local cafe so that he could use the bathroom after they had dropped me off.

The rest of the questions about my life were more banal but equally annoying and I answered each one perfunctorily, counting the seconds until I could jump out of her smelly car and escape her spitting son and her tactless stupidity. Janice was lost in boutique-buying heaven and didn't seem to notice that my monosyllabic answers to her mother had an edge to them. 'Any boyfriends, Ruby? Did your outfit for the Disco Ball cost more than Janice's? Do you like being an only child?'

I bolted out of the car with a terse 'Thank you' the instant her car pulled to a halt outside our wrought-iron gates.

A dark hollowness came over me as I unlocked the large gates then secured them quickly behind me.

I looked up at our white-shuttered two-storeyed house. The purple bougainvillea clinging to the outside trellis.

The honeysuckle climbing wildly up to the second floor like strands of a fragrant necklace. There was music coming from an open window somewhere upstairs and my eyes wandered upwards. It was then that I caught sight of her, my mother dancing, swaying gracefully to the strains of a piece of music that I recognized. It was Vivaldi's *Four Seasons*. I knew it well. 'Music is the right hand, Ruby, and art is the left. The one helps the other. They are equal parts of what makes creative perfection,' were Mother's words when I grumbled about being dragged to classical symphonies when I was younger. She let me miss some, but never Vivaldi. Vivaldi was her favourite.

Suddenly another person came into view through the upstairs window. I stood mesmerized as he wrapped a hand round Mother's slim waist while his other laced her delicate fingers through his much larger ones. She smiled up at him before leaning her head against his broad chest. I dropped my handbag, my keys and my new purchase on to the ground and stood frozen by what I was seeing. He dipped her backwards and I watched as she threw her head back and laughed. I took in a breath of icy air that filled me with sweet honeysuckle and Vivaldi and knew that this was a moment I would hold inside me forever, a cherished nugget of gold. My parents. Swaying together as one, soft light playing on his familiar face as he looked down at her with sheer adoration. She raised her small, pointed chin and gazed up at him.

Here was my amulet of protection against the outside world. The right hand holding the left, the melding together of all that was solid and yet so fragile in these times of hatred and fear. 'Your mother's gallery is under investigation . . .' Mrs Harris's prying words rang through my head and jolted me out of the moment. As I picked up my belongings and made my way inside, the dark, hollow feeling washed over me again.

'You had a phone call while you were out.' Mother's dewy face appeared in the kitchen a few minutes later. She hummed the last strains of the symphony as she poured herself a tall glass of lemonade and offered me one. 'A girl named Loretta phoned. Do we know her, darling? She sounded Afrikaans . . .'

'She's a girl from Steunmekaar,' I answered quickly, and felt a jolt of lightness returning to my being. 'Did she say when I should call back?'

Mother held the cool glass against her check and traced a finger along the tiled kitchen counter top. 'I'm not sure it's such a good idea, darling, to be making friends with an Afrikaans –'

'Mother!' I slammed my glass on to the table. 'You're joking, right?'

'I'm afraid not . . .' she said each word slowly and apologetically. 'Ruby, they hate us, they're watching our every move.'

'They? You mean all Afrikaners? Not just the police and the Special Branch?' I raised my voice angrily.

'Ruby, listen . . . you just met this girl.' Mother came towards me and touched my shoulder, but I shook her hand off. 'You don't know who her parents are, what they do . . .'

'She's just a girl. But she's an Afrikaans girl, that's all, Mother.' I bit down on my lower lip.

'I know this sounds awful, especially coming from me.' Mother frowned, making tiny, feathery crease marks between her arched brows. 'But we're under such scrutiny and with Julian's exhibition weeks away – if there is still going to be one – I just don't need to be worrying any more than I already am. You understand, darling?' She looked anxiously at me.

I could feel simmering anger brewing inside as she spoke, but what came out of me surprised us both. I laughed. An uncontrollable sound that would not stop even when my father, freshly showered, came into the room.

'What's the joke, ladies?'

'She's upset,' Mother said.

'Hardly seems to be.'

'She is. Trust me. It's about the Afrikaans girl.'

I caught my breath, short-circuiting the sound that emanated from me and turned to Father. 'You agree?'

'These are difficult times, Ruby. We need to close ranks, not open our world to strangers.'

'Hypocrites! Both of you.' I shook my head. 'Acceptance of some but not others? What happened to "all men are created equal"?' I circled them both in a slow dance of my own. 'Or is it selective? Black and white but not English and Afrikaans.'

'Ruby, stop!' Father raised his hand to silence me, then turned to Mother. 'Annabel, she's right. We can't bring her into this. She's made a new friend. We've raised her to not see race or creed or colour. It's bad enough she can never bring anyone home.'

'Risk is not what we need right now . . .' Mother ran a quivering hand along her slender neck. 'But I suppose, yes, well, I'm afraid we have lost ourselves in all this.' Mother shook her head. 'What was I thinking? She's only a schoolgirl, yes, nothing more. I've just become very wary and cautious lately,' she said quietly, and sat down slowly at the kitchen table. 'Very, very cautious . . .'

'Is the gallery under police surveillance, Mother?' I pulled up a chair beside her.

'Yes. Every day.' She sighed. 'They lurk around outside the gallery. Go through our rubbish. Sometimes they even send one of their plain-clothed chaps in, pretending to be an art lover.' She closed her eyes and pressed her hands to her temples as if the thought of it all brought on a nasty headache. She rubbed her temples for a few moments, then, as if something heavy had lifted inside, she opened her eyes and held my gaze. 'But I'll be damned if that will stop me from giving Julian his exhibition.' She shot defiant blue eyes at me. 'Even if it has to be at midnight!'

'Brilliant idea.' Father came up behind her and massaged the back of her neck.

'I was planning on telling Julian tomorrow, but with all the uncertainty . . . Now I am sure. A midnight exhibit it will be!'

'The detectives have to sleep sometime,' Father chuckled.

*

I raced upstairs to call Loretta. I was usually home and answered the phone when Loretta called and we had spoken a few times since our meeting several weeks ago, always sliding into our half-English, half-Afrikaans jargon.

I was getting to know her better and from our conversations I learned that her mother had died when Loretta was five from malaria that she had contracted when she swam in an Eastern Transvaal stream filled with infected mosquitoes. Loretta told me that she could not understand why only her mother was bitten when the whole family had been swimming in the water together. Her father said they bit into her because her blood was sweeter than anyone else's. Loretta wished her mother had been less of a good person, then perhaps she would still be alive. She was raised by her father, who she said was very strict. She had an older brother but didn't say much about him, only that they didn't spend much time together.

I lay back on my bed, dragging the long phone cord with me and dialled her number, which Mother had written down on a piece of paper. I didn't need it – I had memorized Loretta's number already.

After five long bleating rings the phone was answered by a young man.

'*Gooie aand.*'

'*Gooie nag.* Um. Is Loretta *tuis, asseblief*?'

The voice on the other end switched immediately to perfect English. 'Yes, of course. She is home. And may I tell her who is calling?'

Was my Afrikaans accent really all that bad, I thought, as I stumbled through an answer.

64

'Um, it's *haar vriendin*, I mean, um, her friend Ruby.'

'Oh yes, I have heard about you. One moment. Yes?'

As soon as Loretta came on the line I kicked my shoes off and lay back on my soft quilted bedspread and relaxed.

'*My broer.* My brother. Sorry if he was rude.' There was a clattering of dishes in the background as she spoke.

'No, actually he was very polite. *Werklik*, his English is perfect.'

'*Hy wou* overseas *gaan* for university,' Loretta said, '*Askies*, but I'm washing the dishes. Servants' day off.' I could hear her turn on the kitchen tap.

'Really, why does he want to go overseas?'

She paused, then seemed to turn the volume of the water up till it almost roared into my ear. She must have cupped her hand round the phone as she spoke because her words came out loud and clear against the torrent. '*My pa* and my brother, they don't get along. They are very different. *My pa, hy is baie kwaad*, angry *met* Boetie.'

I sat up suddenly. 'Why is your father angry?'

Loretta turned the water down and sighed, clattering dishes as she spoke. '*My pa.* He is a real Afrikaner. His grandfather, *hulle* fought *die Engels* in the Anglo-Boer War. My grandfather, how you say, he is one from *Die Broederbond*. You know who is they?'

'No,' I answered quietly. Here it was. The reason my parents feared bringing strangers into our lives.

Loretta said the next sentence quickly and in one breath: 'They show support for Hitler in World War Two. They want *al die swart mense*, the black people, to be kept down by fear.'

65

'Does your father feel that way too?' I asked, feeling the blood leave my face.

Loretta closed a cupboard door. '*Nee*, no, but he wants them never to be equal with us white. *My boetie*, he don't agree. He fight with my father a lot. They both make life hard for me . . .'

'*Ek is jammer.*'

'No, don't be sorry for me.'

A voice from another room called her name. She held the phone against something, but I could still hear the conversation.

'*Loretta, maak jou huiswerk klaar en kom doen jou tuiswerk,*' a harsh voice yelled.

'*Ja pa, ek kom!*' She held the phone to her mouth again and spoke quickly. 'My father says time for homework.'

'Okay,' I said, feeling disappointed that our conversation was already over.

'*Jy is my nuwe vriend*, Ruby. Goodbye.'

'*Totsiens.* You are my new friend too, Loretta.'

As I hung up the phone I wondered if there were an Afrikaans word for 'pal' but, somehow, with Loretta the word '*vriend*' sounded just right.

Chapter Ten

Julian was both terrified and elated by the news of his upcoming solo exhibition. The date had been set for the first Saturday in June, a mere three weeks away.

Mother had told Julian the good news over dinner and I had heard him coughing and rolling back and forth in his bed down the hall all that night. In the early hours of the morning I slipped into my blue silk robe that hung on a hook behind my bedroom door and padded down the hallway in pink bunny slippers to his room and knocked quietly on the door. I too was having a hard time sleeping.

Julian seemed relieved to see me and we made our way in the watery early morning light to the outdoor studio. The golden daffodils that grew in neat rows on the pathway towards the studio ducked their honeyed heads as we brushed by them. A glossy starling chirped a weak shivering note in the crisp cold air.

Julian held the studio door open for me and bowed slightly. 'After you, madam,' he said with mock gallantry. Once inside, the comforting smell of paint and putty and the closed-in-all-night warm air of the studio relaxed me, but apparently not Julian. He paced the linoleum floor back and forth, worrying about every brush or pencil stroke on every one of his works. Was the sketch of the wide-eyed children in the rickety bed too muted in shades? Did the image of the washerwoman with the billowing mounds of clothing balancing precariously on her head evoke enough sense of the heaviness of her load? Did the spittle in the image of the drunken miner lying in the gutter look like vomit instead of drool? He mumbled and paced and I paced beside him just to keep him company.

'They will hate it because there is no happiness in any of them!' Julian shoved his hands into the pockets of his hooded sweatshirt.

'No, they won't. Your work is beautiful.'

'Hah! Your mother's words. That is what she says. But what do you say, Ruby?' Julian stopped and turned me round to face him.

I took one of his large calloused hands in mine and turned it over so that his open palm faced upwards. The pale light skimmed off the surface of his warm brown skin. I ran an index finger along one of the deep arched lines. 'Ah, Mr Mambasa. I see that you will have twelve children in your future.'

Julian smiled down at me and put his other hand on his hip. His teeth were straight and ever so white but I rarely saw his smile.

'I am sorry,' I retraced the line with my hand. 'It is twelve chickens, not children. My mistake!'

Julian laughed. I felt his fingers relax as they rested against my free palm.

'Ah, but look . . .' I traced my finger along a shorter

line. 'This is a line broken in some places but it remains unbroken after a point. Halfway through 1976 it is smooth until the very end.'

'And what is its meaning, O gypsy girl?' He was enjoying the game.

I looked up at him straining my neck so that my eyes met his. 'It means that after a very difficult journey you are now on an easier path,' I said, without lowering my gaze. Then, as if tracing my finger on a letter in Braille, I felt for the deepest cut from the *tsotsies'* blades, a sunken scar on the soft flesh of his index finger. I touched it lightly, then ran my finger deep into its crevice and held the length of my finger inside it. There was a pulse of life in the hollow of its deadened nerve endings. 'This, Mr Mambasa, now this is a rare thing,' I said softly, my eyes never leaving his face. 'It is a sign that success will soon be yours. And your name will be on the lips of everyone in South Africa one day.'

Outside the studio window the glossy starling, warmed by the fast-growing sunlight, shook off his earlier shivers and let out a high-pitched chirp that was loud and strong and full of promise for a beautiful day. Nothing could have been further from the truth.

Thandi reached Mother at home just before she was getting ready to leave for the gallery. I was standing beside her, packing my satchel for school.

'Ousie! Ousie!' Thandi wailed through the receiver so that even I could hear her desperate cries. 'Baas is gone. The *bleddy bliksem* police . . . they handcuff him, they throw him in the van. They tear his nice black shirt . . .'

69

'Thandi, wait. Slow down. Who is taken away?' Mother held the cup of coffee that she was drinking over the sink and mindlessly began pouring it down the drain. Gone, gone, gone. The rich smell of French roast filled my nostrils and suddenly filled me with a sick, heavy feeling inside.

'Baas Dashel, they catch him right as he walks into the gallery. He tried to push them off.'

'But on what charges?' Mother sat down slowly and put her head into her hands. 'The Immorality Act! Oh God, but on what grounds . . .?' Mother was quiet as Thandi spoke. 'I see. I see.' Her foot bobbed up and down in its soft leather mule.

Keep things normal. Normal, I thought, so I finished preparing an egg-salad sandwich, then wrapped it in foil and put it into my satchel. I probably wouldn't eat one bite of it at lunchtime. Janice or Clive would polish it off. My stomach squeezed in an accordion-like spasm. I knew what an 'act of immorality' meant. When I was fourteen, I had heard some of the boys at school talk about going to jail if they got naked with a black woman and got their 'willy' inside her dark '*doos*'. I had gone home and asked Father what they meant and he had told me about a law that was passed in 1950 by the South African government that was simply called the Immorality Act.

'It means that nothing sexual can happen between a black person and a white person. It is, by their beliefs, considered wrong, against the law . . . illegal and both people will go to jail if they are caught.' Father had seemed pained to share this information with me. 'Ah, the joys of living in our country.'

70

'But what if you fall in love with someone of a different colour, Father?' I had asked.

'Darling, Ruby. You cannot. Love is not allowed between a black person and a white person.'

Now my head spun with new thoughts. Was it a black man or woman that Dashel was caught with? Everyone knew that Dashel was homosexual. A *moffie* as the boys at school would say, a sick-o man who liked men instead of women, but to me he was the ever-charming Uncle D.

Mother repeated the phone number that Thandi was giving her over the phone and wrote it down. 'Thank heavens he's being held at the Rosebank police station and not downtown at the Fort.' She paced the kitchen floor, absently wrapping the long phone cord round and round her arm until there was none left to wind.

Father spoke often of the Fort. It was a place where prisoners wept when they knew they were going there. Many times they went in and never came out. Accidental death was usually the reason given.

I went upstairs and put my school uniform on. White shirt. Blue pinafore. Normal. School tie. Normal.

Then I went downstairs and told Mother that I wanted to go to the police station to see Dashel, but she insisted that I go to school. 'There's nothing you can do, Ruby, so go and learn something useful. And don't worry. I reached your father and he is already on his way to the police station.' She smiled weakly at me but I could see the concern etched in the lines around her mouth.

I rode my bike faster and faster until my legs spun

round in lightning fury. And as I whizzed past the green trees and the manicured lawns I saw the coils of the phone squeeze tighter and tighter round me and Father and Mother and Julian and Dashel and the gallery and Thandi. My breath seized and I gulped for air like I was suffocating in their coiled grip. I fought the urge to stop pedalling but the need to ride, ride, ride kept me in frenzied forward motion. *Ride*, my body commanded. *Ride far away from a world as harsh and as cruel as this one.*

In record time I was at the school gates.

Chapter Eleven

It was hard to concentrate on Mejevrou de Jager's lesson on Afrikaans expressions and idioms that would be important for us to use in the composition portion of our upcoming exam. Images of elegant Dashel with a torn shirt and behind bars kept flashing before me.

'*Smoor verlief* – does anyone know what that means?' Mejevrou tapped the word she had just written on the chalkboard with a majestic flourish from a long sharp stick as if the answer would magically appear in a puff of smoke and hang there in mid-air beside her elaborate scrawl. It was no surprise that thoughts of magic and spells came to mind in her class. She had ratty black hair and a long pointed nose. She always wore black.

'Anyone?' She scanned the silent room with her dark owl-like eyes. Her sharp stick stopped at the sight of one single raised hand.

'Monica. Yes, what does it mean?'

I felt my body tense at the sound of her name. She sat a few rows in front of me to my left and although I could not see her face I could hear the dreamy lilt in her voice. 'Well, "*lief*" means love . . . and "*smoor*" means smeared or mushy.' She giggled and flicked her long blonde hair back. 'So I guess it means mushy in love.' She turned her head sideways and stared directly at Desmond, who over the past few weeks had moved seats so he now sat directly to her right. She held his gaze and giggled again. Desmond grinned and blew her a kiss and the whole class tittered.

'Correct!' Mejevrou de Jager rapped her desk with her stick in delight. 'Mushy or completely in love. When we are head-over-heels over someone we do become completely like melted butter. Yes?'

There was a general murmur and titters of agreement from the class.

I tried to imagine who could possibly make witchy Mejevrou de Jager feel soft and giddy, but before I could entertain any further thoughts about her romantic life she rapped loudly on her table. 'Pay attention, class.' She spun round and aimed the point of her stick at no one in particular. 'There is a very important change about to take place in this country. It has to do with the Afrikaans language. Does anyone know what it is?'

There was a choked silence in the class.

'Anyone?' She opened her owl-like eyes wide and scanned the room. No volunteers were forthcoming. There was a long silence and then she pointed the stick at the one raised hand in the classroom.

'Ruby, yes?'

My words came out slow and tight, as if the poisonous idea could barely leave my lips. 'There is talk that the government is going to pass a law that will make all the black schoolchildren in Soweto and in every township and at every school learn all their lessons in Afrikaans instead of English.' I mumbled the next sentence under my breath. 'Even though most of them don't speak Afrikaans at all.'

'Very good, Ruby, but the last part that you mumbled, about them not speaking the language, is exactly why they need to learn Afrikaans.' She circled closer to my desk and I lowered my eyes so that I did not have to look into her hard stare.

'Yes, class, Afrikaans is just as important as English and it is high time it was also the language used by the Bantu.'

No one reacted to her use of a derogatory term, Bantu, for the blacks. But apparently no one in my class cared to know or understand anything about what black people wanted.

I felt suddenly very alone in this school of perfect white teenagers who were so flawed by their ignorance. Surely there must be a teenager like me somewhere. But where?

I had listened to Father and Julian's concerned discussions about this horrendous law that the government was about to enforce.

'What will they think of next?' Father had slammed his fist on his desk when Julian had told him of this looming possibility. 'Imagine, Ruby, one day you walk into your school and are told by your teachers that all your lessons and exams will be in Japanese – and you don't speak a word of it!'

'The talk in Soweto, I hear from everyone, is that the children, they will not do it. Even the little ones, eight or nine years old. They say they will not learn in the language of the oppressors.' Julian lowered his head, 'The government, *hai*! They want Afrikaans to remind us every day that we belong to them. Even the language that we must read and think in.'

'There will be bloodshed.' Father shook his head. 'I fear that blood will flow.'

'I'd fight,' I said, 'if suddenly I had to be taught in a language I didn't know.'

'They will not,' Julian said. 'They are young and poor. They are the offspring of parents who are maids and miners who bow and scrape in the presence of a white man. They let themselves be called "boy" or "girl" even when they are grown men and women. These young children in the townships, their parents will put their fear into them.' Julian had shaken his head and sighed.

As we filed out of Afrikaans class and made our way to the biology lab Clive caught up to me. He was fast becoming my other good pal and he, Janice and I were definitely becoming a visible trio at school.

'Hey, how'd you know about all that stuff?' Clive carried his book bag in front of his chest with one arm and pushed his glasses up on the bridge of his prominent nose with the other.

'I read the newspaper,' I answered quickly.

From behind came a voice from one of the Desmond followers. They were sauntering behind us with their leader in the middle. They sped up and closed the gap till I could almost feel the fast-paced clacking of their well-heeled shoes on the hollow corridor.

'Hey, Ruby, how's your family? Been hearing lotsa bad

things about them lately. Like trouble with the law. Huh?' one of the boys shouted.

'Yeah, you know about all this political rubbish, 'cause they're bleeding communists!' another added.

'A red commie, hey that's why they named her Ruby . . . Ruby Red!' Desmond suddenly whooped.

'Yeah, Ruby Red!' they jeered in unison.

Thoughts flooded my mind: *Don't speak. Run. Ride. Fly. Anything. Just get away. Fast. Don't answer. Don't say a word. Protect. Close in. Shut down. Think about something calming and something thrilling.* I forced my head to fill with images of Julian and Johann Duikster, back and forth, back and forth. The faces of understanding and exhilaration. The wonderfully known and the achingly unknown. I walked faster and faster with Clive's bobbing books and curls keeping up beside me.

A sudden jolt of pain as something was thrown at me from behind.

'Leave her alone!' Clive spun round as a plum hit the back of my head.

I could feel its juices drip down through my hair and on to my neck but I didn't flinch. I didn't want to show that I was affected by them and their hateful actions despite the dull throb that pulsated in the spot where the fruit had landed. My eyes stung and a flame of something new, something indescribable, began to burn inside me.

'The black-loving commie is bleeding red!' one of them chortled, and they all laughed just as the bell rang for the beginning of the next class.

*

As we got to the lab I asked Mr Morrison, the biology teacher, if I could be excused. From the sour look on his pock-marked face I could tell that he was about to say no so I quickly added, 'A female issue, sir,' which I knew he would not challenge.

He gave me a terse nod and I hurried down the empty corridors to the girls' bathroom.

Once I'd made sure I was alone in the bathroom I went into one of its grey disinfectant-smelling stalls. The tears came hard and fast. I tried to stop them but they had a mind of their own and ignored my feeble attempts to dam them up.

What flooded over me was a feeling more than humiliation at the hands of Desmond and his friends, more than doubt about how I would cope with finishing my final school year, more than the fact that my family's beliefs were being questioned and judged. What I felt was truly alone at Barnard High.

Janice was sweet and Clive tried to be understanding when I explained that no one was allowed to come over to our house. But the truth was they did not know me. Really know me. No one did.

Although we had only met once and she was a class behind me at school, the girl I felt closest to was Loretta. There was a creeping understanding and openness in our half-English, half-Afrikaans exchanges on the phone.

As I splashed cool water over my face and took a paper towel to my sticky neck and hair I felt suddenly brightened by the thought of the plans that we had made for the upcoming Saturday afternoon. Loretta had invited me over to her house, and Father had agreed to drive me there. Since his and Mother's initial objection, they now both seemed more than obliging to help get me and Loretta together. A joint show of support for my new Afrikaans friend. And 'black-loving commies', as Desmond called them, had to treat everyone as equals.

As I made my way back to the biology lab I heard a distant sound, the low put-put of a lawnmower outside. Through an open window at the end of the corridor I caught sight of the old gardener in his floppy flower-adorned hat methodically mowing the furthest school lawn. He seemed intent on the task and I wondered if in his world of seeds and flowers and fertilizer, he knew of schoolchildren being forced to learn in a language they did not speak or understand. Did he simply live in his meagre back room on the school property and never leave, or did he travel every Thursday, the unofficial day that most servants and black workers had off, to Soweto to visit his children and grandchildren, who cried to their old Papa that their lives at school were soon to change for the worse.

'Miss Winters, why are you wandering the corridors and not in class?' A stern voice came from behind me. I turned round and was face to face with our school principal.

'M-Mr Dandridge,' I stammered, 'I had to use the girls' . . .'

'Well, hurry on then, no dilly dallying. You're a prefect and prefects have to set a good example.' He raised a chubby hand and shook his finger at me as if he were reprimanding a small dog. He waddled away in his ill-fitting navy suit. I took a deep breath before entering the biology lab and straightened my school tie. It was askew, like everything else in my life.

I got through the rest of the day with no further incident, but I could barely focus on the rest of the afternoon classes. Dashel's arrest filled my every thought. Who had caught him? And where? Dashel was not ashamed of being homo-sexual but I also knew that he was very discreet and careful. He never flaunted his romantic life and the few men I had met with him at gallery openings were always introduced to us as 'my good friend Basil', or 'my close friend Brian'.

Much as I tried to reassure myself that Father was handling everything, I jumped from my seat and raced to get my bicycle as soon as the last bell rang. I pedalled fast to the one place I knew I could get an answer.

The Rosebank Police Station didn't look much like a place of incarceration. Perhaps because of its location in one of Johannesburg's posh northern suburbs, it had been designed to hide – camouflaged with its modern design and the circular fishpond, well stocked with giant orange koi fish. Once inside there was nothing modern or pleasant about it. Stark white walls, a row of benches where a few people sat huddled in groups. They were mostly black. A weathered wooden counter with a partitioned glass window that was now closed. A sign read RING/RING, which was the same in both English and Afrikaans, so I rang.

After a few painfully slow minutes the window was opened by a young red-haired woman in plain clothes. I could feel her taking in my private-school uniform. Her eyes rested on the Barnard school crest on my blazer.

'Yes, miss, what can I do for you?'

I felt the sick feeling squeeze tight like a rubber band in my stomach again. I had to stop myself from wincing. 'My uncle, I am here to find out where he is . . .'

'Was he arrested?' she asked, tapping her pen lightly on the countertop.

'Yes, this morning . . . his name is Dashel.'

She smiled. 'Ah, but, of course, the charming Mr Dashel Bryant. He kept us all very entertained.'

'Entertained?'

Entertained was the last word I had conjured up for Dashel all day. *Frightened. Hurt. Bewildered* and *humiliated* were the ones that I had imagined.

'Yes, he had us all in stitches with his stories; he even invited me to stop by the gallery before he left.'

'Left . . .?'

'Yes, miss. All charges were dropped.'

'Dropped?'

'Miss, are you okay? You seem a little . . .'

'Fine, I'm fine.' I shot her an unconvincing smile.

'Perhaps a glass of water? Yes?' She disappeared into a back room before I had a chance to object. I steadied myself with one hand on the countertop. The rapid shift from absolute dread to sheer relief was wreaking havoc with my senses.

I downed the glass of water in one gulp and thanked

the red-haired police lady behind the counter and was quickly on my bike again. The news that Dashel was safe and not behind bars filled me with elation and I whooped and shouted like I had when I was eight or nine and something had made me full of glee. I sat far back on the bike saddle and lifted my feet off the pedals, waving at everyone I passed by. Some of them waved back with a strange look on their faces. I must have appeared ridiculous but I didn't care. For once nothing mattered except that Dashel was safe and probably back with Mother and Thandi, sipping tea at the gallery, which was where I was now headed.

As I coasted down Jan Smuts Avenue I remembered the words that had been jeered at me earlier in the day.

'Your family's in trouble with the law,' one of Desmond's cronies had shouted.

'Trouble with the law' was something that was said to a tanned cowboy by a sheriff with a shiny badge in a Wild West film.

Ruby Red. That's what they had called me and, yes, that's who I was. Ruby Red. Outlaw. Bandit. Desperado.

I swung my legs off, patted my bike and swaggered through the gallery entrance, leaving my spurs outside.

Chapter Twelve

The first sound that reached me as I walked through the oval maze of galleries was laughter. It was coming from Mother's office and was punctuated with the tinkling sound of glasses clinking together. It was reassuring to be able to identify each reverberating voice. Mother, a low soft chuckle, Father, a deep full-bellied bellow, Dashel, a high-pitched bray and Thandi, a roller coaster of earthy guttural tones that were punctuated with loud knee slapping. I paused in the office doorway, suddenly reluctant to go in, wishing I could bottle their joyous sounds in a beautiful porcelain jar. Something wonderful to open and inhale, like sweet perfume, when laughter was nowhere to be found.

'The policeman was so sure that she was on her knees doing the act. I mean, if I hadn't had the needle and thread hanging from my trousers button . . .' Dashel downed the last drop of liquid in his glass as I walked in. 'Ah . . . here's our very favourite girl. Come join the celebration.' Dashel put an affectionate arm round me and pulled me in for a hug. 'Uncle D is free!'

Mother came over and kissed my cheek with a flourish.

'I called the school to give you the good news . . . did you get the message?'

'No,' I said. 'I worried all day . . . Can someone please tell me what happened?'

Thandi shimmied towards me, her coloured hair ribbons rippling like jellyfish tentacles on her shoulders. She took my hands in hers and tried to get me to dance with her but I wasn't budging. She smiled at me, revealing the large gap where her two front teeth should have been.

'Baas Dashel is home getting dressed to come to the gallery. The house maid, Sookie, is fixing his trousers because the button broke.'

'But he's wearing them, his trousers, you see.' Father filled Dashel's empty glass again with champagne.

'And, dahling one, what none of us knew was that your dear Uncle D was being watched, spied on with binoculars by a rather handsome and muscular policeman.' Dashel swirled the champagne in his glass dramatically before taking a delicate sip.

'They've had Dashel under surveillance too,' Mother explained.

'Too?' I said. 'Not just the gallery?'

Thandi sat me down on Mother's plush apricot couch and handed me a fluted glass. I shook my head – it was already swimming, floating in unexplained bubbles with giant question marks inside their orbs.

'I don't understand. Why was he arrested and then let go?' I looked from Mother to Father for an explanation.

'Because what the handsome policeman thought he saw was a black woman kneeling down in front of me, a white

84

man, performing fellatio, when all sweet Sookie was doing was kneeling to sew a button back on to my trousers!'

'Fellatio?' I asked.

'Oral sex.' Father coughed and looked down.

'The policeman's binoculars only saw the naked top half of my body. He barged right in just as Sookie was done sewing, and arrested us both, with the telltale needle and thread still hanging from my lower region. Ghastly – the whole thing was just ghastly!' Dashel put a hand to his forehead. 'He tore my shirt after he made me put it on because I fought off being handcuffed. The uncouth brute!'

Father finished the details of the story while I sat on the couch with my head on Uncle D's unbruised shoulder. It felt good for us all to be together in Mother's quiet gallery and I wished that Julian were here with us. Then our unconventional family would be complete.

Father explained that while it was punishable by law for a white man and a black woman to be engaged in any sexual activity, they literally had to be caught in the act. The exuberant young policeman had raced into Dashel's bedroom because he assumed that what they had been doing was breaking the law. When questioned by his superior officer at the police station about the details of what he discovered, and with Father throwing every legal ploy at the now nervous young man as he tried to build his case, he confessed that he had not seen anyone unclothed. When Dashel showed 'handsome policeman's' superior the dangling needle and thread still attached to his fly button, they were forced to release both Dashel and Sookie, who was being held in a different part of the station reserved for black prisoners. It took several hours of paperwork before they were released, so Dashel passed the time entertaining the police station clerks. Dashel told us that when he was uncuffed and handed back his belongings he could not resist a parting comment to the arresting officer.

'I looked him straight in his face and told him that I, Dashel Bryant, confirmed homo, would never do anything sexual with a woman no matter if she was black, white or purple!'

'*His* face went quite purple, I daresay!' Father added, and we all laughed.

Over the next few days the relief that Dashel and Sookie had been freed in a country where suspects could be held without reason or cause for months and even years subsided. What began to sink in was the harsh reality that we were under police surveillance everywhere. It was not just the gallery and Dashel's house in the quaint suburb of Norwood that were cloaked in the dark shadow of scrutiny. We now became aware that the police had stepped up their security forces and were watching us from outside our house, waiting to see who came and went and what possible illegal activity was taking place in our suburban home. They lurked in the lobby of Father's office building and probably even, I suspected, followed me as I went about my life.

I rode to school every day that week no longer enjoying the winding roads and lush foliage but with one eye constantly looking, scanning beside me and behind me to make sure that no one was cruising slowly in an unmarked car watching my every move. Sometimes I felt their ominous presence fixing their steering wheel on my moving form and I would ride recklessly, dodging through traffic and swerving round pedestrians to try to get away. In those desperate moments to escape, Ruby the Outlaw took over and I imagined the dust cloud that would billow up behind me and choke them as they tried to close the gap. But my wild pony outsmarted them every time.

Chapter Thirteen

The Saturday visit to Loretta's could not have come soon enough. It had been a dreadful week with Mother snappy and anxious and constantly gnawing on the corners of her nails, which was most unlike her. Julian seemed irritable and frustrated since he had been advised by Mother and Father not to leave the house until after the exhibition was over for fear he would be picked up by the police on some false charge that would put him behind bars until after the show. He spent most of his time brooding and pacing and painting in the studio and declined hot chocolate late at night when I knocked on the door and asked if he wanted any. Father looked haggard and tired and spent many hours in his study with the door closed on whispered phone calls that he said he hoped weren't being tapped.

School was equally bad, with Janice out with the flu she had caught from her whiny brother, Gerald. Clive's parents had suddenly let him know they would be getting divorced right after he finished high school and he was planning on failing every subject just to keep them together. Monica had even tried to speak to me in the tuck-shop queue but I had turned and walked away before she could get very near. A traitor was a traitor. I ate lunch all that week with a very glum Clive at the furthest end of the empty rugby field.

I made daisy chains out of fallen dry pine needles while Clive swore off ever getting married and having children. The promise of Saturday was the bright light at the end of the bleak week tunnel.

Late on Saturday afternoon, Father drove me through the unfamiliar streets of Randburg in virtual silence for the first fifteen minutes. I knew that, while he had decided to be agreeable about my newfound friendship, it was still worrisome to him.

'So her father raised them alone?'

'Yes. Their mother died when Loretta was five.' I toyed with the smiley appliqué that was sewn on to my denim bellbottoms.

'And she has an older . . . brother, is it?' He looked in his rearview mirror for the umpteenth time. I knew he was checking to make sure that we weren't being tailed.

'Yes, he's a year older. Matric. Like me.'

'And her father does what, exactly, again?' He gripped the steering wheel and made a sudden turn on to a wide tree-lined street called Hans Strijdom Drive. 'Damn, almost missed it.' Father glanced down at the directions Loretta had given me earlier that day.

'He has an architectural firm that does mostly government developments,' I said quickly, regretting instantly that I had mentioned the word 'government'.

Father snorted. 'Ha! Government work . . .' then shook his head.

89

I wanted to apologize for Loretta's father but I wasn't quite sure why, so I said nothing, and we rode the last few blocks to her house in silence.

'Here we are, five-six-five-three Groenwald Road.' Father turned into a circular driveway and stopped in front of the flat-roofed single-storeyed beige house.

I felt my pulse jump against the elastic gathering of my cheesecloth smock top. 'Yes, here we are.' I took a deep breath and planted a quick kiss on Father's cheek. 'Thank you. Really.'

Father gave my hand a squeeze. 'I'll wait for you to go insi–' Before he could finish his sentence, Loretta opened the front door and smiled her big warm smile.

As she made her way down the grey slate steps to Father's car I thought how much prettier she was than I had remembered. Perhaps it was the floral sunshine-yellow dress that swung loosely from her tall frame or perhaps it was just that everyone looked better out of school uniform, I did not know, but what I did know was that warmth radiated from her no matter what she was wearing.

'It is my pleasure to meet you, sir.' She put her hand through Father's open window and shook his hand. I noticed that our phone conversations had definitely started to give her an ease with English that she did not have before.

'Likewise.' Father flashed her a smile and a look of relief crossed his face. 'I'll be back at nine to get Ruby, if that's okay?'

'She is welcome for any time as she wants.' She caught her mistake quickly, '*Askies*, I mean for as long as she wants.'

'Thank you, Loretta.' Father put the Citroën into gear.

As he pulled out of the driveway Father turned back and waved. I was glad that he had met Loretta and hoped it would calm his anxiety about my new friend.

Loretta held both my hands in hers. 'You are here. *Ja?* I cannot believe . . . yes. Finally! Come.'

We climbed the large smooth-stoned stairs together and I felt happier than I had in a long time.

As she opened the front door the smell of steaks cooking on an outside *braai* filled my nostrils. 'Boetie, I mean, my brother, he is cooking up some steaks and *wors* for our supper. You eat meat, yes?'

'Oh yes!' I reassured her.

As we walked through the contemporary-designed house I noticed the lack of a woman's touch. Most of the rooms were carpeted in dark chocolate brown or dark tile and the living room was dominated by large, oversized leather couches that surrounded a heavy oak rectangle coffee table. There was a zebra skin stretched out in front of an unlit fireplace and an ivory elephant tusk jutted out above the mantlepiece. My eyes were drawn to a heavy panelled cabinet in the dining room that was filled with gleaming silver trophies.

Loretta followed my gaze, '*Ja*, those are mostly Boetie's. He's a big athlete. Soccer, rugby, swimming. *Alles!* You will meet him soon. *My pa*, he is still at the Country Club.'

I went with Loretta down a wide tiled corridor that had paintings hanging on both walls. Being the daughter of a gallery owner I found myself examining the art in other people's homes scrupulously. Loretta's father, in contrast to their ultra-modern home, chose traditional oils that showed scenes of the history of his Afrikaans forefathers. As we passed through the hallway I glanced for a moment at paintings of Voortrekkers sitting round a campfire, their white-canopied ox wagons in the background, another, a Cape Dutch house nestling against the majesty of Table Mountain, and a third, a ruddy-faced farmer, Bible in one hand and rifle in the other.

'*My oupa*, he gave all this art to Pa before he died.' Loretta made a face. 'Boetie and me, we don't like them, but Pa says out of respect to his father . . .' Her voice trailed off as we came to the door of a room. '*Hier's my kamer. Kom binne.*' Loretta smiled.

She ushered me into her room. It reflected everything that Loretta was: warm and inviting. I was glad there was at least one room in the house that had bright, feminine colours. Her bed was covered with a purple-and-yellow quilt with large black-centred daisies dancing in circular patterns. Her bedroom walls were painted aquamarine, which swirled like sea-foamed waves. I felt as if I had stepped into a psychedelic picture book.

'Gee whiz!' I said.

'Pa is very strict with *alles*, but he was very good about letting me make this room the way I want it.'

She positioned herself on the edge of her bed and I sat down in a plush purple beanbag that faced her nightstand. On it was a single item. A silver-framed picture of a striking blonde woman leaning against the trunk of a large tree. Her blue dress was cinched tight into her small waist and her hair lay pale and wispy against her angular cheeks. On her hip she held a toddler, a little blonde girl who had her downy head resting in the curve of the woman's neck.

'*My ma*,' Loretta said softly.

'I'm sorry.'

'No worries. It was a long time ago.'

'You were so young when she died.' I shook my head.

'What is your mother like?' Loretta plumped the pillows as if her hands needed something to do.

I was caught off guard. No one had ever asked me that question before, nor had I ever thought of how to sum Mother up.

'Well, she's lots of things.' I imagined Mother in the gallery as she talked earnestly to an artist, her small hands undulating in the empty air. 'She's passionate about art and artists. She likes to help other people. She's very beautiful . . .'

'She sounds much excellent.'

I did not correct her choice of words. In many ways Mother was just that. Much excellent.

'We have our moments,' I added, but in truth those moments were few and far between. I knew how lucky I was to have a good relationship with my mother and how many of the girls at school disliked their mothers and felt distant from them.

'I wish *my pa* had married again,' Loretta said wistfully. 'He says no one could ever . . . what is the word in *Engels*? Place over Mother?'

'Take her place,' I said.

'Yes, take her place.' Loretta and I were quiet for a moment, our eyes resting on the image of the little girl in her mother's arms.

Loretta turned and looked at me. 'I am very happy you are here.'

'Me too.' I smiled back at her and in that moment all the dreadful things from the week faded away.

Loretta hopped off the bed. '*Kom*, let's go and see if Boetie needs help with supper.'

I followed Loretta down a maze of corridors until we reached the back door. A shiver went up my spine as she opened the door and the cool air rushed in. The garden was lit with torched lanterns and dominated by a kidney-shaped swimming pool.

'Boetie!' Loretta shouted out. '*Kom, my vriendin Ruby is hier!*'

At the far end of the garden, beyond their swimming pool, was the figure of someone leaning into the burnished flames of the *braai*, intently focused on what he was doing.

'Boetie!'

This time he cocked his head at the sound of his sister's voice and turned in our direction. The glowing light from the flames caught the gold of his hair and it was in that moment that I recognized his body movements, the sureness of his actions. He turned, waved and put down the large fork that he was holding in the same hand that I had last seen with a rugby ball in its grasp. The world stood still.

Johann was 'Boetie'. Johann was the brother I had spoken to on the phone but never knew. How did I not know?

Johann, who was now smiling and walking towards us. My heart leaped with the flames that glowed behind him.

He extended his hand and I felt myself tremble as his fingers and palm touched mine. 'Ruby. It is nice to meet you.'

'Yes,' was all I could get out, then, 'Very.'

'Loretta said that you were very pretty and for once she did not lie.' His hand held mine for a second longer before releasing it and I felt the instant loss of his touch.

'Thank you,' I stammered. 'I saw you win against our school.'

'I told you she was *lekker mooi*!' Loretta punched her brother's arm affectionately. 'And I don't lie, Boetie!'

'My sister's English is much better since she is your friend,' Johann said. 'She hated studying it before – *ja, sussie?*'

We walked back around the pool to the *braai*. I could barely hold myself steady on the grassy lawn and felt light and giddy. I stumbled on a sprinkler head and Johann caught my arm. 'You okay?' I felt his fingers cup my elbow.

'Yes.' I said breathlessly. 'I'm fine.' But the truth was I was more than fine. I was wonderful.

It took a half hour for me to stop marvelling at the impossible. That this was real. That Johann Duikster was talking to me and putting *boerewors* and steaks on to a platter for us to eat together.

We moved into the kitchen and I helped Loretta set the breakfast-nook table while Johann arranged the meat and corn that had been boiling in a pot on the stove on to plates. Their servants apparently took Saturdays off instead of Thursdays. The phone rang and Johann came back to say that their *pa* had called to say that we should start without him. He was running late at the golf club.

Our conversation over dinner drifted from one subject to another and I soon found that Johann had the same warmth and ease as his sister. We talked about the latest music from England and America. The Rolling Stones and the Eagles were favourites of Johann's while I liked Carol King and Fleetwood Mac. Loretta was a big fan of Abba and announced that Olivia Newton John was worth having a poster of on the wall. I looked over at Johann a few times just to make sure he was real and I hadn't just conjured him up from wishing too much. He caught my eye and held my gaze just long enough for me to feel a warm flush wash over my cheeks before I looked away. Loretta must have been aware of the quiet flirtation that was going on between our bites of sweet corn and juicy steak.

'Johann, he says that all the *meisies* at our school are boring –' she glanced over at her brother with a wicked grin – 'but the girls, they all chase him anyway.'

Johann laughed. 'They just like the idea of me – captain of this and captain of that. Like a prefect badge that they can wear on their school blazer.'

'Ruby is a prefect.' Loretta began clearing the table.

'Me too,' Johann said. 'Something in common, yes?' He looked over at me.

'Yes,' I said, and I felt myself swimming deeper and deeper into his liquid blue eyes.

The slamming of the front door with a loud smack broke the moment.

'My *pa* is home.' Loretta turned to Johann. 'No fighting, Boetie, okay?'

'My father and I do not, how do you say, see eye to eye,' Johann added.

I didn't have a chance to respond because Meneer Duikster's deep voice filled the room. It was followed by the sour smell of whiskey.

'*Aangename kennis.*' He slurred slightly as he spoke. He took me in but did not extend a hand. He was a tall man, well built with a short, cropped goatee. His head was completely bald but, despite the lack of hair, he was a youthful-looking man, probably close to the same age as Father in his mid-forties.

I stood and practically curtsied to him. '*Aangename kennis, Meneer Duikster,*' I said in my most perfect Afrikaans, and tried not to breathe in the alcohol fumes. Neither Johann nor Loretta seemed to be aware of the strong smell that surrounded him and I wondered if it were something they had grown used to over time.

Loretta jumped from her seat and went to the kitchen to prepare a plate of food for her *pa*. The warm, relaxed mood that had permeated the room quickly evaporated. I felt my hands grow hot and clammy and my throat tighten so that not another word could get out. It didn't seem to matter because Meneer Duikster did not look at me again, nor direct any questions at me. He ate methodically and seemed lost in a post-afternoon-drinking haze. He asked a few questions in Afrikaans to both Johann and Loretta mumbling words between mouthfuls so that I could barely understand anything that he was saying. Something about rugby practice for Johann and a question for Loretta about a shirt he needed the servant girl to iron on Monday. Johann answered his questions tersely but gave me a few apologetic smiles and asked if there were anything else I wanted to eat. All I could do was shake my head. I watched the hard, set lines of Meneer Duikster's mouth and saw that despite the slow slurred manner of his speech there was a coldness to his words. It was obvious that neither Loretta nor Johann took after their father. Their kindness and warmth came from the soft beautiful woman in the picture frame who was long gone. I watched Loretta, suddenly keyed up and on edge as she tried to make light conversation with her father. How was his golf game? Did he want to lie down after dinner?

She also tried to fill in the blanks of Johann's monosyllabic answers to their father. It was obvious that she played middleman between them. Meneer Duikster seemed kinder and gentler towards her, if that were possible.

He stood on unsteady legs and pushed himself away from the table as soon as he was done eating. He gave me a half-nod as he passed by me.

I felt my throat relax and open again once Meneer Duikster was gone.

'*Askies vir Pa.*' Loretta began clearing away his dish immediately, as if to rid the table of the sourness that he had left in the room. 'Saturday is his day for golf and whiskey.'

'He is . . . what do you say . . .' Johann swirled the lemonade in his glass. 'A piece of works.'

'Piece of work,' I said.

'He is not always so bad.' Loretta lowered her eyes. 'I am sorry. I should have met you somewhere else . . .'

'But then I would not have met Ruby.' Johann cocked his head at me, his blond hair falling forward and I felt my heart lurch and hurtle into my stomach.

Loretta smiled and looked from me to Johann and back again. 'Well, for this I am glad then,' she said slowly, and I felt the warmth in her eyes again.

Chapter Fourteen

Sunday went by in a blur. I walked through each minute on dreamy air. Light and fluffy feelings drifted through me like soft white clouds with Johann at the centre of each one.

I helped Mother hang paintings for the exhibition. I rewrote my essay for English literature about whether love was inherently tragic. I changed my point of view and said that of course it wasn't!

On Tuesday night I posed for Julian in the studio. He had decided that he wanted one portrait, something completely in contrast with his other work. He must have felt guilty for ignoring me all week so, to make up for it, he invited me to be the subject of his last painting, the one that would complete the collection. It was to be a statement piece. A vision towards change, even though Julian felt that change would be a long time in coming for his people.

'You are fidgeting too much, Ruby.'

'Why do I have to wear my school uniform?' I complained.

Julian had asked me to wear my winter school uniform, blue pinafore, white shirt and school tie, including the blue panama hat that none of us girls ever wore. He had me sit in a straight upright chair with a book in my hands. I was to pretend to be reading it intently. When he told me what he wanted, I did not see the significance of the painting. A white schoolgirl reading a book did not seem to be a subject that would draw any attention.

'What's so great about me reading? I don't get it.'

'Look at the cover, Ruby.' Julian had set up his easel a distance from me and had already begun sketching.

I turned the book over and looked at its cover. He had put a false cover on the book. It was obvious that Julian had painted the jacket cover and the title carefully. The title was in a language I did not know.

'*In-kul-uleku!*' I said guardedly.

'*Inkululeku!*' Julian pronounced the word for me. 'It means "freedom" in Xhosa,' he said, without looking up. 'One day white children shall learn to read in our languages, just like we have to learn theirs.'

'Brilliant!' I said.

'Now will you stop complaining?' Julian gave me an impish grin.

I sat still in the chair holding the book and did not move for at least twenty minutes. I wanted so badly to tell Julian all about Johann, but knew that now was not the time. He needed absolute concentration and quiet when he began a new work. Once the initial pencil sketch was down and the paintbrushes were brought out I would be free to talk but, for now, I had to be patient so I opened the book.

Julian had been devouring all the books on our book-shelves since he had moved in. Several were piled high on the nightstand in his room. He must have taken one from his growing mound and redressed it with his own jacket design. I opened the book to a page.

'Read to me,' Julian said.

'But you like quiet . . .'

'I will make an exception. This book is about finding inner peace and a higher purpose.' His eyes glanced up and held mine for a second.

'Shall I read from anywhere?' I asked.

'Yes. It is all good. It is a book about a seagull.'

I opened the book and began reading. '*For most gulls, it is not flying that matters, but eating. For this gull though, it was not eating that mattered, but flight. More than anything else, Jonathan Livingston Seagull loved to fly.*'

'A big thinker, this bird is,' Julian chuckled. 'Read on . . .'

'*"Why, Jon, why?" his mother asked. "Why is it so hard to be like the rest of the flock, Jon? Why can't you leave low flying to the pelicans and the albatross? Why don't you eat? Jon, you're bone and feathers!"*

'*"I don't mind being bone and feathers, Mum. I just want to know what I can do in the air and what I can't, that's all. I just want to know."*'

'Knowledge.' Julian's fingers moved smoothly across the canvas. 'That is what life is all about, Ruby. A yearning to understand and achieve something beyond our limits.'

'In a country full of limits,' I sighed.

'Ah, but, like Jonathan, we must learn to fly above them.'

I looked at Julian and felt a sudden flood of adoration for him.

'How are you so wise?' I asked.

Julian shook his head. 'I am not completely sure but I do know that suffering snuffs out our youth and sharpens our senses.' Julian looked back and forth from me to the image that he was creating.

'You are a wonderful subject to paint, Ruby.' His eyes grew soft as he held the charcoal ever so gently on the canvas image.

'Julian, there is something I want to tell you.' I riffled the pages of the book on my lap.

'Yes, I know.'

'You do?'

'Yes, it is about a boy.'

'How did you know?'

'It is in your eyes, Ruby. They are the outside windows to our hearts. What people learn about our hearts is open to them through our eyes, yes?'

'I suppose.'

'There are velvet curtains hanging in your window.'

'That obvious?'

'Yes, for me.'

'What about your window?'

'Filled with knotted branches. No view past them into my heart until after the show.'

'It's going to be wonderful.'

'That is what I am most afraid of,' Julian said quietly. 'Tell me about this boy that has stirred all this sparkle in your eyes like sugar in a glass.'

'He is very kind and special. I think he might like me too.' I felt my cheeks grow hot.

Julian put the charcoal down. 'You can stretch now.'

I stood and arched my back and reached my arms high in the air.

'Is he in your class at school?'

'No, he goes to another school. Steunmekaar.' I yawned and held my arms out wide.

'Afrikaans.' Julian said the word slowly and frowned. 'One from the camp of our oppressors.'

'Julian, he is not like that! Mother and Father had a problem with me having an Afrikaans friend at first, but he isn't that way . . .'

Julian dug his hands deep into his pockets and looked down at his feet. He shook his head. 'I don't need you here any more, Ruby. I will finish the painting from memory.'

'Julian. Don't do this. He isn't a bad person,' I pleaded.

'Ruby. Please leave. I need to be alone.' Julian's voice was terse and clipped. He would not look me in the eye but focused on the ground and rolled his heels back and forth in his worn moccasins.

I pulled off my panama hat so fast that its elastic strap snapped against my chin. I felt my eyes sting as I fought back tears and ran from the studio, a seagull in flight who thought that being different was okay. That stretching my wings open wide was what they had wanted me to do. Mother, Father and even Julian. But there were rules to be obeyed in their pristine air. Rules that on the outside claimed that acceptance of others was what was most important. But here they were. Hypocrites! Selective acceptance, according to their 'open-minded' beliefs. The very beliefs that had isolated and alienated me from my own peers. My head pounded with purple rage as I raced up the stairs to my room to call Loretta. The only real friend that I had.

It was Johann who answered the phone. He recognized my voice instantly. Clearly not too many English *meisies* called their house.

'Ruby,' he said, sounding pleased to hear my voice.

I felt my breath sucked out of me as he said my name. 'Um, yes, Johann. Um, I was . . . is your sister home?'

'No. Not yet but I will tell her you called.'

'Okay. Thanks,' I wanted to hang up the phone. I needed to calm myself. Julian's anger and now Johann on the other end of the line. 'Bye,' I managed to get out.

'Wait!' he said suddenly. 'Ruby. Don't go. I would very much like to see you again.'

'Yes.'

'I am sure that you are always in big demand with the boys at your school. Being so beautiful . . .'

I practically choked.

'But would you do me the honour of letting me take you to a drive-in movie this Saturday night?'

A kaleidoscope of brilliant colour washed over me and I steadied myself by clutching the post of my bed. Turquoise. Violet. Emerald.

'Saturday?' I whispered.

'Yes, this Saturday, unless you would rather not . . .'

'No! Yes. I mean yes, of course!' I took a gulp of psyche-delic air. 'It's just that it is my school's annual dance, our Disco Ball.'

104

'Another time then . . .' Johann sounded disappointed.

'No, Johann, I mean, you can come with me, as my da– . . . Um, we are allowed to invite someone from another school to join us . . .'

'A disco ball –' Johann chuckled – 'sounds like fun. We have a very formal annual school dance. Tuxedos and ball gowns.'

'Ours is pretty different.' My voice had finally found its way back to normal but I still gripped the bedpost. The colours swirled.

'That sounds very nice. I accept the invitation. Thank you, Ruby.'

'Johann.' I suddenly panicked. 'You will probably be the only Afrikaans person there.'

'That's okay. I can take care of myself. And you, of course, on Saturday night.'

My hands could barely hold the receiver steady.

'But what do I wear?' he asked.

'Something you can dance in.'

Johann laughed. 'Very well, a pink tutu it will be!'

We hung up after I gave him directions to our house and told him that seven o'clock on Saturday night would be perfect. Johann was eighteen and had his driver's licence and I was sure that Mother and Father would not object to him driving me to the dance once they had met him.

I lay on my soft carpeted floor and felt a kaleidoscope of emotions to match the swirling colours.

Yellow fear. Blue sadness. Orange joy. A bitter-sweet coming together for, in finding Johann, I was losing Julian.

Chapter Fifteen

With the exhibition the following week, I spent every afternoon after school helping to get the gallery ready. Thandi and I counted all the RSVPs to the midnight inaugural showing and well over two hundred guests were coming. Word was spreading fast through the art world that this new young artist from Soweto would be the emerging bright star from the dark world of the townships. Mother had invited a number of art critics and patrons, prominent black political activists as well as well-to-do whites from the northern suburbs. The combination would be ideal, she had said, and word was that people were clamouring to get a personal invitation. Mother always hand-picked the crowd and would not budge when it came to who was and who was not on her list. It was not out of some sort of snobbery that she screened each and every invitee. She needed a safe crowd, with as close to an assurance as she could get that no police informers would show up unexpectedly. She usually kept the number of guests coming to a manageable size but Julian's upcoming exhibition seemed to have taken on a sizeable life of its own.

'Thandi, Ruby, Dashel!' Mother yelled from somewhere

in the gallery, her voice reverberating and bouncing off the oval gallery walls in long, rounded syllables. 'Meeting in my office, pronto!'

When we were all assembled, Mother went over the plan for the evening for the hundredth time that week. Drinks and hors d'oeuvres would be passed around as well as champagne and wine. There would, of course, be the 'fake trays', as Mother called them, which would be stacked neatly in the back kitchen and ready to go, if the unpleasant and unlikely need arose. The 'unpleasant situation', as she called it, was a police raid. Since the crowd of patrons would be an illegal mix of blacks and whites, the black patrons would all quickly be handed the 'fake trays' to carry, as if they were staff and not guests, if the police suddenly descended on the gallery. There was, of course, nothing illegal about a black person passing hors d'oeuvres around at a party. The task of handing out the trays fell on Thandi, me and Dashel. We had experienced a raid once before during Dumali's exhibition opening last year and had hurriedly passed the trays off without a hitch, but it had been an unnerving and frightening few minutes that I hoped would never happen again.

Mother was about to go over the introduction of Julian at the opening. He was to step out at an appointed time from a side gallery into the Gallery Grande, but her instructions were interrupted by the sound of heavy-soled boots trampling across the quiet gallery floor. The footsteps stopped for a moment before continuing. Then a man's voice echoed through the gallery.

'Is anybody here?' he bellowed.

Mother sighed. 'Not now, whoever you are . . .' she said under her breath.

'I'll go.' I rose from the plush couch and headed in the direction of the man's voice.

I found him in the small first gallery. His back was turned away from me as I approached. He was staring at an abstract painting of a tap dripping water. The artist, a well-known eccentric who took inanimate objects and transformed them into sexual parts of the body, had developed a huge following and Mother always carried a few of his works in the gallery.

'Is this what I think it is . . .?' he asked, without turning round as I approached.

He was a tall man with broad shoulders and wore a light khaki suit.

I had learned from Mother never to explain what a particular painting meant, but rather to draw the interpretation out of the patron so that he or she felt engaged and competent in their own assessment and understanding of what they were looking at. Art was, Mother always said, purely subjective.

'What do you think it is, sir?' I asked politely. He turned and looked at me. Dull grey eyes and short black hair that looked stark against his pasty white face. He had an upturned nose set over a thin mouth.

'You look a bit young to be working here,' he said accusingly.

'My mother owns the gallery.'

'And she lets you look at filth like this!' He wagged his finger at the wall.

'It's a tap,' I said.

'Like bloody hell it is. It's a man's private parts hanging out there for everyone to see.' He snorted.

I felt the familiar accordion-like squeezing in my stomach and bit down hard on my lower lip. 'Is there something in particular I can help you with, sir?' I said in a polite but firm manner.

'No, just looking, just looking around.' He clasped his hands behind his back and began moving through the gallery, stopping at each painting, squinting, then stepping close up to them. Sometimes he sniffed the air around him or scratched the back of his neck before moving on to the next painting. I followed at a respectable distance behind him. I wished that Mother or Dashel would come to my rescue but neither appeared. Mother often left me to deal with visitors to the gallery and I had even made a sale or two of my own in the past.

'Very interesting, yes . . .' he said, scraping his heavy boots across the spotless floor and leaving dark-soled imprints. 'Lots of black artists show here, am I right?' He stopped in front of a canvas of a boy standing beside a rickety bike, his tattered clothes blending into the rubble and smokestacks of the township behind him.

'Some,' I said. 'Sir, is there any artist in particular that I can interest you in?'

'All.' He moved on. 'I am interested in all. Especially the black ones.' He spat the word 'black' out like it had a bitter aftertaste.

My stomach squeezed tighter, a sickening feeling filling

my insides with a horrible certainty. I was face to face with an undercover policeman.

'Exhibitions?' he said. 'Any coming up that I might want to attend?'

'No,' I said curtly.

'You sure? I had heard there was one just round the corner . . .' He shook his head. 'Funny . . . I must be mistaken.'

'Yes. You are.' I took a deep breath.

'What's your name?' He turned his dull grey eyes on me and I felt them boring into my head.

'Ruby,' I said. 'Ruby Winters.'

'Well, Ruby, you tell your mother that she has a very clever daughter and that, if she's as smart as you, she'll do what's best for her gallery.' He gave me a thin smile. 'For her daughter's sake.' He turned on his heels and strode out of the gallery. I stood transfixed, unable to move a single muscle, my eyes blurring on the tarnished marks that his sturdy boots had left behind.

That night after dinner I told Father about the incident with the undercover policeman in the gallery. Julian was conspicuously absent from the meal and I was afraid that the reason he was not there was because of me rather than a painting he needed to work on, which is what he had told Mother earlier.

'Cancel! Absolutely not, David!' Mother tried to raise herself above her petite stature to meet Father's eyes. 'Julian has worked too hard for this. I will not let fear and veiled threats affect my life or the operation of my gallery.' She placed her hands on her hips and looked up at Father who turned and walked towards the liquor cabinet in the living room and poured himself a drink from a cut-crystal carafe filled with amber liquid.

'They know about it, Annabel. They'll raid. There'll be arrests or worse . . .' He downed the drink in one quick gulp and slumped into a brocade-covered chair.

Normal. Keep things normal. Talk about school.

'I got an A in my history test,' I said brightly, but neither one was listening.

'This is so not like you, David. The man I married said that he would never back down. That we had to live and maybe die for what we believed in.' Mother stormed over to his chair, her face just inches from his.

'That was before . . .' Father said.

'Before what?' Mother raised her voice.

'Before Ruby. Before we had a child, Annabel,' Father said softly.

Mother stood slowly and turned to look at me. It seemed she had not been aware of my presence in the room until that very moment. She blinked once or twice as if she needed to get me in focus.

'Ruby, darling. You understand, don't you? You've been such a big part of all this. You've become Julian's muse. And look at all the time you've put in at the gallery for the exhibition . . .' Her voice trailed off as her eyes filled with tears. 'The show must go on – you understand.' Her voice quavered. I stood unmoving even though she opened her arms wide for me to go into. It was her artists that mattered most to Mother. I just had not realized it until that very moment.

'Yes, Mother. The show must go on,' I said, and turned away. Father's angry words followed me as I ran up the stairs, two at a time, to my room.

'Well, I'm not condoning this one, Annabel. Blast it! You're putting us all in jeopardy. Including your star Julian!' He must have thrown the tumbler down hard on the floor for the sound of glass shattering rang out behind me as I fled.

I lay on my bed and listened to the melancholy whistling note of a dikkop bird outside my bay window. I remembered Father telling me once that some people believe its plaintive drawn-out notes are a sign of misgivings, but he thought its notes were hauntingly beautiful. I felt the chill of the night air and tried to hear the same pleasing sound that Father found from the little bird, but I could not.

Julian's show, I knew, would go on and I would not have wanted it any other way. But there was a deep feeling brewing like rain clouds in my centre. It was Father who was my protector against the world. The one who would put nothing before my safety. I felt something inside me burst with pelting pain. I was flooded with the realization that before me was a sea of named and unnamed artists who saw Mother as their shelter while she, in turn, gave them her unwavering commitment to their safety and well being. The picture of Loretta's mother holding on to her so tightly came to me in that moment, and I knew by the protective angle of her arms round her daughter that had she still been alive she would have been Loretta's sanctuary, and would have always put her daughter's safety first.

Chapter Sixteen

With the Disco Ball just days away, school was a veritable buzz of excitement. I had to go to Miss Allison, the school's administrative secretary, to give her Johann's name and to tell her which school he attended. That was the protocol if you were bringing someone from an outside school. She gave me a quizzical look over horn-rimmed glasses when I said the word 'Steunmekaar', but I was ready for the onslaught of snide remarks and comments. There was no one I would rather be bringing to the dance than Johann.

With each passing day at school I felt more and more alone. Those who had originally stood by me in the 'Desmond and Ruby standoff' seemed to have deserted my camp and only Clive and Janice were my school companions now.

'I can't believe it!' Janice practically jumped into my lap when I told her who my date for the ball would be. 'He's the grooviest! Ohhh, I can't wait to meet him.' She danced around me, swaying her hips, the pine needles popping and crunching beneath her feet. We had taken to spending lunch break at my new favourite spot, which was at the far end of the rugby field. Since my encounter with Desmond and his gang I preferred eating as far away from the rest of my class as I possibly could.

Clive, who lay stretched out on the grass, was a lot more concerned about my choice of partner for the ball.

'Jeez, Ruby, you'll have more than a plum thrown at you!' He shook his head. 'It's not just that he's any boy from Steunmekaar, for heaven's sake, he's the captain of their rugby team. All the boys at our school know who he is and what he looks like.'

'He's the captain of the swimming team too.' I punched Clive on the arm teasingly.

'It's not funny, Ruby. C'mon, you used to be the most popular girl at school and now you go out of your way to be the most unpopular . . .'

'Ouch! That was mean.' Janice gave Clive a stern look. 'Ruby doesn't care what other people think.'

'Well, maybe she should start caring . . .' Clive kicked at the ground, sending pine needles scattering in all directions.

'You don't have to be my friend, Clive, if you don't want to . . .' My throat closed around the words as if the pine needles had stuck there.

'Of course I want to!' He threw his hands up in the air, his curly hair bobbing wildly. 'Look, I've never been a part of the "in" crowd. I've always been a bit of a misfit.' He plonked down on the ground beside me. 'But you, Ruby, you've always belonged. I'm sorry. I guess I don't quite understand why it doesn't bother you.'

'She has us.' Janice sat down next to me and put her arm round me.

'Yes, she does.' Clive did the same. 'You two are like my new family –' his voice faltered – 'since my real one's falling apart.'

I put my arms round them both and we sat there, holding on to each other for just a brief moment, while across the field I could hear the distant sound of laughter and excited chatter from the rest of our class. I wished that I could tell Janice and Clive that the truth was I had never really felt that I was a part of the popular crowd. I wished too that I could share with them the description of Julian's painting of me and the upcoming midnight gallery exhibition, but I couldn't. And, as I let them go, I felt a sudden sadness for what would never be. Open words without hidden secrets. It was no wonder that I didn't feel the loss of popularity. It had been a burden I had carried around for a long time, a tiresome responsibility instead of a source of joy and a pleasure. Popularity had meant hiding the truth from a greater number of people. A constant ducking and diving behind excuses and flimsy explanations. Yes, my father was a lawyer. Yes, my mother owned her own business. Yes, we led normal suburban lives just like everyone else, except no one could come over and no one could ever know our real truth.

Even Monica had never fully known me, I realized sadly.

I looked from Clive to Janice and back again. My loyal pals. 'You two are the best,' I said, and meant it.

As I rode home after school, I thought about Loretta. I had been worried that she might not take kindly to me inviting Johann to the dance, and I feared that my newfound friendship with her might suffer now that her brother had my attention. But I was quite wrong. She had called me later on the very night that I had spoken to Johann and was delighted to hear that I had invited her brother to go with me.

'*Hy hou van jou!*' she said with an excited lilt in her voice.

'I like him too,' I said sheepishly.

'Then, for me, *alles is goed*!' Loretta laughed.

'Yes, everything is good,' I said.

'Johann asks for me what flowers you like best. I say I don't know.'

'Daffodils but they're off season. Lilacs are always wonderful.'

'Boetie is, how you say, picky with the girls. But you are special.'

'So are you, Loretta.'

I said a silent thank you that this kind girl had come into my life when I most needed her.

Julian was standing in the driveway when I rode in. He looked gaunt and tired, his eyes sunken back in his strong-featured face. He wore rumpled jeans and a paint-splattered white T-shirt.

'Come,' was all he said as I got off my bike.

I quickly dropped my satchel inside the house and followed him.

We walked silently down the path to the studio. I wanted to say something light and conversational but the words would have fallen on deserted ears because he suddenly strode ahead of me.

I felt my pulse quicken with dread and anticipation. The memory of how our last encounter in the studio together had ended was still painfully fresh in my mind.

Julian was already at his easel when I entered. He was standing with one hand protectively holding on to a corner of a white drop cloth covering the painting beneath it.

The empty space between us felt rigid. The air seemed to slink away into the cracks of the studio walls until Julian finally spoke.

'Not a second has gone by since you were last here that I did not feel pained by my behaviour, Ruby.'

'It's okay,' I said softly, walking towards him.

'No it is not.' His voice crackled with emotion. 'You were not deserving of my anger.'

'It doesn't matter . . . as long as you aren't angry now.'

'I have been tortured by this . . .' He lowered his head.

'Don't, please . . .' I hugged him tightly. He leaned against me and clutched me fiercely.

'My God, you're burning up!' I felt molten heat radiating from the core of his being.

'I am ashamed of my actions.' He clung to me even tighter. 'Forgive me.'

I breathed in the acrid smell of paint and unwashed skin and felt the harsh scraping of his unshaven cheeks against my shoulder blade but I did not pull away. I was glad that I could be there with him and relief washed over me that I had not lost him.

'It's all right,' I whispered against his ear.

He heaved a deep sigh, then slowly unwound his arms

from mine and wiped his damp face on the sleeve of his T-shirt.

'Walk ten paces back, then turn round and close your eyes,' Julian said.

I could feel him watching me as I did as I was told.

With my eyes closed I felt a strange dizzying sensation. I sucked in a deep breath of the paint fumes and Julian's scent that were all around me.

'Open now,' he said.

I opened my eyes. Julian stood with the white drop cloth in his hands, his red-rimmed eyes trained on my face as I took in the painting on the easel. It was a scene of a young boy of perhaps eight or nine, standing with the tin-roofed, makeshift homes of Soweto's shanty town behind him. His clothes were pitifully large and hung like loose elephant skin around his frail dark body. The shirt cuffs drooped from his arms and the oversized dark trousers were bunched in folds round his thin ankles. His naked feet stood on the potholed dusty street. In his barely visible hand he held a purple crayon. The small boy's eyes were raised upwards, beyond the billowing smokestacks that blew foul grime into the desolate late-afternoon skies. But above all the wretchedness hung a pale crimson and gold-ribboned sky where a single white bird with grey-tipped wings flew ever higher, its circular path traced by a swirling lavender trail that was tinged with deep shades of magenta. The little bird was very far from the open azure ocean, but its species was unmistakable.

'It's a seagull,' I said.

'Yes,' Julian said softly.

'And the boy –' my eyes filled with tears – 'is you.'

'It is every boy, Ruby. Every child who has ever dreamed to fly above our dark world into the open skies.'

'It is the most beautiful painting you have ever done.' I felt the tears begin to roll down my cheeks.

'Ah, now it is your turn to cry.' Julian came towards me and gently wiped my tears away with the corner of the white drop cloth that was still in his hand. He clucked softly. 'It must be contagious.'

'Mother will be so pleased . . .' I sniffed.

'It's not for the exhibition. It is for something much more important.'

'But . . .' I began to speak, but Julian placed a finger over my lips.

'It's for you, Ruby.' He moved his finger away and pulled my face towards his and held it between his large rough hands. Deep, dark eyes filled with liquid emotion held mine for a second. Then Julian tilted my head and kissed me gently on the forehead.

'I don't deserve this,' I said.

'But you do, Ruby. More than you will ever know.' Julian went to the painting and took it off the easel and held it out to me.

'It is called Ishiboshwa *takes flight*.'

'What does it mean?' I asked as I took the painting from him.

'*Ishiboshwa* means "the prisoner".'

'The prisoner takes flight,' I whispered. 'I will treasure it forever.'

'Yes, forever.' A pained look crossed Julian's face despite the smile he gave me as he opened the studio door.

I walked out of the studio into the afternoon light and turned to thank him, but he had his back to me, his eyes fixed on the now empty easel.

'Thank you, Julian.'

'Have a good time at your school dance,' he said quietly, without turning round.

Chapter Seventeen

I had tried to keep myself from pacing back and forth in my room but it was impossible. I had counted days, then hours, and now finally minutes until seven o'clock Saturday night would be here, and Johann would pick me up and drive us to the Disco Ball. There were four and a half minutes left to go. I could still not believe that Johann wanted to be my date. We had spoken earlier in the day and, despite his promise that he wouldn't be late, I was struggling to calm myself, but jumbled thoughts kept pulling me in all directions. This was all a big joke that I had played on myself. I was going to the Disco Ball alone. There was no date. No Johann. I see-sawed back and forth between what was real and what was not. In the moments when I believed that it was all true and that Johann would be ringing the doorbell at any minute, I would rush to my vanity table and stand in front of its large mirror and check my hair and make-up for the hundredth time. I marvelled at how decidedly different I looked tonight. Sleek dark-lined green eyes under layers of mascara, shimmering pink lips and shiny dark hair that I had flipped at the ends with a curling iron. I laughed nervously at the face that stared back at me. 'Cleopatra goes Disco' came to mind.

I rarely wore a lot of make-up. But tonight was different. Tonight I wanted Johann to be proud to be seen with me. I wanted Monica to take in my new fitted lime-green jumpsuit and my new white platform shoes and remember all the fun we used to have shopping together. I wanted to be carefree for once. Tonight, I decided, as I ran a blush brush over my cheekbones, nothing was going to stop me from being a normal seventeen-year-old teenage girl with a handsome boy at a dance. Nothing. Neither hateful Desmond nor guilty thoughts about Julian, who had locked himself up in the studio all day and showed no signs of coming out.

It had taken some negotiating with Mother and Father to agree that Johann would be allowed to come into our home to collect me. I had assured them that I would not discuss Julian or the exhibition or anything about our lifestyle with him.

'We have to meet him, Annabel. He'll be driving her, for heaven's sake.' Father shifted his jaw from side to side, a habit that usually meant he was unhappy about something. I wasn't sure what was upsetting him more, a stranger coming into our home, or the fact that his only child would be under the care of another man, even if it were only for an evening's outing.

'Goodness, my daughter looks so grown up!' Mother had stood behind me and fastened a green beaded necklace round my neck. 'I must be getting old. And you, my dear Ruby –' she turned me round to face her – 'are getting more and more beautiful.'

As I nervously made my way downstairs I said a silent prayer that there would be no security police watching our house tonight.

The gate chime rang just as I reached the entrance hall. I buzzed Johann in through the gates and waited to hear the front doorbell ring. I closed my eyes and took a deep breath, and, although I was expecting it, I jumped when the melodic sound rang.

Johann was wearing black slacks and a pinstriped jacket. His blue shirt was open at the neck and a silver cross was visible on his smooth chest.

He took me in appreciatively and I felt the blood rush to my cheeks. 'You look, how can I say . . . out of this world. Great.' He smiled.

'You look great in a tutu!' I laughed and he laughed with me, and as I ushered him inside I felt that everything was going to be okay.

I floated through the brief but pleasant introduction of Johann to my parents. Father seemed satisfied enough to let us leave without firing too many questions at him while Mother was gracious and amiable and seemed charmed by Johann's formal use of the English language.

'I will be sure to have your daughter home before midnight, *meneer*, sorry, I mean, sir.' Johann shook Father's hand on the way out of the door.

'*Meneer* is just fine.' Father gave Johann a pat on the arm.

'*Aangename kennis*,' Mother said in Afrikaans, and I almost toppled off my platforms down the patio stairs as we made our way to Johann's car. It was a language that she despised, for it had only been spoken to her of late by policemen and people who wanted to destroy her and her gallery. I had never heard her utter a word of it before, despite the fact that all English-speaking South Africans had to study it as a second language at school.

I turned to look at Mother, her lithe frame leaning against Father who had his arm round her small waist. She blew me a kiss and in that moment I loved her more than I ever had before.

'Have fun!' she shouted as Johann held the door to his silver Buick open for me, and soon we were on Jan Smuts Avenue on our way to Barnard High.

Johann seemed relaxed and I leaned back on the soft leather seats while he told me about his dream of studying abroad after high school. His athletics would guarantee him a scholarship in most foreign universities. He wanted to get as far away from his father as possible. His father drank too much and had a hard line approach to keeping South Africa a pure-white-controlled country.

'My grandfather was even worse. He was a member of *Die Broederbond*. They beat up blacks and even worse . . . It makes me sick to think about it.'

'You believe blacks should be equal?' I promised myself that I wouldn't talk politics, but it was impossible for me not to ask after his comment about his father and grandfather.

'Yes. It is not a fair way for human beings to live. But I keep this mostly to myself . . .'

'I feel the same way,' I said quietly.

Johann reached over the gear lever and squeezed my hand, leaving his fingers wrapped round mine.

'We have more in common than you think, Ruby.'

I held Johann's hand and, instead of feeling nervous, a calm descended over me. Here was someone who truly thought like I did and cared deeply about things beyond his own world. Something inside me settled, like the ocean holding smooth and still after an eternity of rough seas. I wanted to tell him my secrets. Somehow I knew he would understand.

'We are here, I think.' Johann looked over at me. 'Are you ready?'

Barnard High was lit with roving searchlights that bounced across the quadrangle and up the high brick walls. The rugby field had been converted into a giant parking lot and the music coming from the gymnasium was so loud that it throbbed through my feet as they hit the ground.

Johann took my hand and smiled at me. 'You okay?'

I wanted to turn and run to the far end of the rugby field to my secluded spot and take Johann to sit with me amongst the pine needles away from everyone else. I felt suddenly protective of him, this kind, handsome boy who had grown up without a mother.

'Maybe we shouldn't have . . .' I started to say, but Johann turned me to face him.

'It will be fine. I will not let anything ruin our evening.'

He pulled me towards him and put his arm round me and I felt the ground pulsate and my legs quiver as we made our way into the gymnasium.

The gleaming disco ball that hung from the middle of the room cast diamond shapes across the dancing groups of teenagers. There were several boys in black slacks and open-necked shirtsalready on the dance floor and I was glad that Johann would blend in with the other boys. Neon spandex leggings that hugged every inch and silver and gold hot pants were the most prevalent fashion statement for the girls. My one-piece jumpsuit stood out and I felt glad that dancing was something that came naturally to me. Johann led me on to the dance floor. I felt curious stares from a few of the girls as we wove through the throng.

We danced well together and one of the girls in my class, who was close by with her partner, leaned over and asked, 'Who is he? He's dreamy!'

I was about to answer when Desmond and Monica made their way on to the dance floor.

I leaned into Johann. 'Let's take a break.'

He took my hand and I steered him in the direction of Clive and Janice, who I'd spotted sitting together at a small table amidst silver streamers and white balloons.

Clive and Janice had decided to come to the Disco Ball together since neither one had a date. They were staring down at the two watery Cokes on the table in front of them looking horribly glum. Janice brightened up considerably when she saw Johann and me heading their way.

She stood up and waved, and giggled when I introduced her to him.

'I kept telling Ruby to look at you when you were playing on the rugby field. I spotted you right away,' she babbled.

Johann was patient and charming as she rambled on about how much she loved rugby and what a great player he was. I tried to start a conversation with Clive, but he mumbled a few words and continued to stare vacantly at his Coke. I suggested that we all go and get some food together, but Clive shook his head and Janice, feeling obliged to keep Clive company, remained with him, although I knew from the look on her face that she would have much preferred joining us in the food line.

The ultraviolet lights mounted on the walls of the gymnasium made anything white gleam and shine under their fluorescent brightness. It was fun to watch the students gyrating as they danced, where anyone wearing white shone in blinding neon light.

Johann and I stood in line and I could not help but feel a thrill as he placed his hand on my waist. 'You are the prettiest one here,' he whispered in my ear.

'And you are the most handsome one here.' I reached my hand up and placed it boldly on his strong jaw line.

'Ruby,' someone said, breaking the moment. I turned round to see who it was and my heart sank. It was Principal Dandridge. He had a half-finished plate of salad and chicken in his chubby hand, but was apparently in line for more food.

'The potato salad is a must!' He pointed to the creamy remnants of it on his plate. 'Don't miss it!'

'We won't,' I said quickly, and was about to ask how Mrs Dandridge was enjoying the ball, when he turned his full attention to Johann.

'You look very familiar . . .' he began, speaking between bites of chicken that he shovelled in through his rubbery lips. 'Are you a King Edwards lad?'

'No, sir,' Johann replied, 'I am a Steunmekaar lad, sir.' The chicken practically spewed out of Principal Dandridge's overstuffed mouth. He looked from me to Johann incredulously, the waiting potato salad suddenly forgotten. 'Now I know why I recognized you.' He wagged a fat finger at Johann. 'Johann Duikster, captain of Steunmekaar's formidable rugby team.' He shook his head. 'You're a brave young man to show your face here. Our team doesn't take losses, especially to an Afrikaans school, too lightly.'

'It's a dance, sir,' I said, my voice sounding unnaturally high and shrill. 'This isn't about rugby.' Johann sensed my growing distress and put his arm round me protectively.

'In fairness, sir, we are all sportsmen playing a game . . .'

'I don't want any trouble, Duikster, is that understood?' He shook his head at me as if to say, 'What were you thinking?' and waddled off.

'It's much too early in the evening for trouble,' a voice drawled from behind Principal Dandridge. 'The fun hasn't even started yet.'

Desmond and Monica sidled in behind us and I could not help but notice that she was wearing the exact same jumpsuit as mine. Only hers was in blazing purple.

'Well, lookie, lookie what we have here . . .' Desmond raised his voice above the music. 'A red and a redneck . . .' he goaded.

Johann's grip on my hand tightened, but I forced myself to turn round to face them. I felt a burning charge ignite in me, a fire that had long needed to find release aimed at its much deserving targets.

'A snob and a snake . . .' I said, looking from Desmond to Monica.

'That's so mean!' Monica hissed, and narrowed her eyes.

'A snob . . . I'll take that as a compliment.' Desmond flashed a cunning smile in my direction, then looked over at Johann and eyed him up and down. 'But cavorting with our Afrikaans rival, now that's just plain insulting to all of us at Barnard High.' He sneered at Johann, 'Keep her on a leash. She's a bitch with a vicious bite.'

Johann let go of my hand and grabbed Desmond by the shirt collar; his movement was so swift that Monica let out a terrified yelp. Desmond's eyes bulged from the tight grip Johann had on him.

'Don't you ever insult Ruby ever again, *jy hoor*?' he said in a deep, quiet voice, his face just inches from Desmond's.

Monica and I stood silently glaring at each other.

Within seconds Johann was hauled backwards by six or seven boys. The unexpected attack from behind forced him to release Desmond from his fierce grip, and Desmond catapulted back, knocking over the precious bowl of potato salad behind him, before slumping forward, gasping for air.

'Kill the bloody Afrikaner!' he yelled as soon as he'd found his voice.

A veritable roar went out amongst his gang, and they all rushed Johann, knocking him to the ground.

Monica glared up at me from her crouched position next to Desmond. 'Now let's see what becomes of you, Ruby!' she spat venomously at me.

In that fleeting instant I looked at her guarding Desmond protectively, flashing her almond-shaped eyes at me with pure hatred.

Best friend. I once had a best friend. A long, long time ago, or so it seemed.

How high does a bird have to fly before the noise of the city below fades to blissful silence? How fast do its wings have to flap until it cannot see the land below? How many miles must it travel until its past seems distant and the future glows pale and shimmers up ahead? That was what I wished on the evening of the Disco Ball. To be that bird, carried far, far away on lofty winds that embraced me and transported me away from all the hurt and humiliation of that night. A night where Johann was punched as many times as a boxer in a ring, a night where Principal Dandridge demanded that once I had cleaned up Johann's bloody lip and eyes in the boys' bathroom, with he himself standing guard outside the door to ensure that there would be no further incidents, we were to leave immediately. A night where, as we exited the gymnasium with Johann coughing uncontrollably and leaning heavily against me, Principal Dandridge informed me that I was to turn in my prefect badge first thing on Monday morning.

I barely heard his words for by then I was already flying, circling high overhead, his strident voice fading further and further away as I pulled Johann and I into the safety of his Buick.

We held each other in the dark leather confines of his car. His pinstriped jacket was shredded from the elbow down, his trousers stained with the blood from his fresh cuts.

I did not know the words, nor could I find the voice to tell him that it was all my fault. My blind stupidity of wanting him to be with me, to be my date at a school dance, where acceptance of anyone from the outside, least of all a rival Afrikaner, was not tolerated by teachers and students alike. I alone had brought this upon him.

Johann groaned and leaned back on the seat, his blonde matted hair falling forward. 'I don't think they liked me much . . .' he chuckled. He reached for my face and ran a finger gently though my hair.

A half laugh, half cry came out of me. 'I'm so sorry . . . Johann, will you ever forgive me?' I took his fingers and held them to my lips. He lifted my bent head and pulled me towards him. 'I have been wanting to kiss you all night . . .' he whispered, then touched his swollen lip, 'but with this . . .'

'Nothing is impossible . . .' I leaned in and pressed my lips ever so gently against his. He reached for the back of my head and pulled me in even closer.

'You are the most . . .' he began, but our lips locked against each other so that he did not get a chance to finish his thought. We clung to each other, inhaled each other, with every kiss deepening, with every touch more ardent, with every caress more intoxicating.

Johann's desire for me lit up a longing. A loneliness. A wanting to feel alive, a purpose for striving and seeking and achieving. A yearning for acceptance of all that I was, the open and the hidden.

Is there always that one kiss that makes us feel that we have finally arrived? It was not my first kiss, but it was the only one that mattered.

We flew that night, Johann and I, higher and higher, to a place where there were no longer boundaries that kept us separate, English and Afrikaans, boy and girl. We were, in those moments, or perhaps they were hours, in the darkness, as one.

Chapter Eighteen

Dr Jacobs was used to being summoned by Mother to our house in the very late hours of the night to deal with an emergency of one kind or another, but he could not hide the shocked look on his face when, instead of a dark-skinned wounded man to tend to, he found a strapping eighteen-year-old white boy. And an Afrikaans one to boot. He was a true gentleman, and spoke quietly to Johann in Afrikaans as he sewed up his split lip and the deep cut above his eye, while Mother went in search of some clean clothes in Father's closet for Johann to change into. I held Johann's hand while Dr Jacobs applied a stinging salve to the newly stitched skin.

Father hovered outside the guest bathroom door and insisted on following Johann in his car all the way back to Randburg just to make sure Johann did not faint at the wheel from loss of blood.

'I have been beaten up just as bad on the rugby field, Mr Winters,' he told Father once he was dressed and ready to go.

I could feel Mother's eyes on me as I brushed a lock of hair out of Johann's eyes. She seemed jumpy and nervous, and I knew that they were waiting for an explanation of what had happened at the dance once the three of us were alone.

But I needed time by myself. To relive the night. To soak in all the earlier horror and all that later filled me with indescribable happiness. I needed time to relish and revel in the bliss that was Johann, but also to mourn the loss of all that had once been mine at Barnard High.

I was a true outcast now and I did not want to think about what Monday morning at school would bring.

Once Johann and Father had left, with Johann giving me a quick kiss on the cheek, since both my parents were watching, and telling me that we would talk tomorrow, I said a most sincere thank you to Dr Jacobs and a quick goodnight to Mother and bolted upstairs to my room.

Julian's painting was the first thing I saw as I entered my room. It was carefully propped against the wall next to my large window, waiting for Father to hang it tomorrow. I had invited Mother and Father up to see the painting earlier in the day and as they gazed upon the extraordinary depth and meaning of the work, they were both speechless. I knew Mother would really have loved to include it in the exhibition, but she said that it was a special gift from Julian to me and it most certainly would be bought if it were put out in public view.

'I will never give it up,' I told her ardently.

'Of course you wouldn't, darling. No one is suggesting

that you do . . .' She had reached for my hand to reassure me.

'I think he's your most talented artist yet, Annabel.' Father stood admiring the painting and nodding his head. 'Yes, I do believe you have a real winner on your hands . . .'

I lay on my bed and looked into the upturned eyes of the little boy in the painting, but it was the purple crayon in his hand on which my eyes settled and remained.

'Well, young Julian, can you help me draw my way out of this mess now?' I whispered in the semi darkness.

I fell asleep waiting for him to answer.

Chapter Nineteen

I did not ride my bicycle to school on Monday morning. Nor any other day that week, as it turned out. The weather had turned bitterly cold and I had come down with a terrible sore throat.

Mother gave me lots of honey, lemon and hot water to drink before Father drove me to school on that dismal Monday morning. They had both been horrified to learn about the events that had occurred at the Disco Ball and were far more upset than I was about my impending loss of status as a prefect. Father, being the lawyer that he was, had demanded an audience with Principal Dandridge. It was granted for 7.15 a.m., fifteen minutes before the school day began.

I coughed and spluttered and blew my nose, waiting in the corridor outside Principal Dandridge's office on a hard wooden bench that sent wood slivers through my tights like biting red ants every time I shifted position. Occasionally I could hear the calm but raised voice of Father, but could not make out the exact words.

Father emerged ten minutes later looking ashen and visibly angry.

'I had no idea that you'd been excommunicated from your crowd. That there's some sort of hate-hunt going on.' Father ran a large hand through his hair. 'Blast it, Ruby, why didn't you tell us? I had no idea . . .'

'You and Mother have had other things . . .'

Father knelt beside me and grabbed me by both arms. 'You are the most important thing in our lives, you hear?' he said fiercely. 'You, Ruby, no one and nothing else.' He put his arms round me and I could feel his body tremble. 'You're not a prefect any more. Dandridge won't budge.' He held me tightly against his freshly ironed cream-coloured Oxford shirt. I could smell the Old Spice aftershave that he splashed every morning on to his just-shaven face.

'It's okay, Daddy,' I said, and patted him on his broad back as he held me close. 'It really doesn't matter any more.'

He released me then and looked at me through misty eyes. 'Daddy. I haven't heard you call me that in a long time.' He pulled me to my wobbly feet. 'Nasty cold for a nasty day.' He shook his head. 'Dandridge said for you to go in.' He reached inside his jacket pocket and handed me his monogrammed handkerchief: *DAW, David Adam Winters*. I took it gratefully from him and turned in the direction of Principal Dandridge's office.

'I'm proud of you, Ruby . . . don't ever forget it!' he called after me. I could not see the pain in his face because my back was already turned, but I could hear it in his unsteady voice.

'As I am of you, Daddy,' I whispered.

My father's handkerchief got me through the day. I clutched on to it as I handed back my prefect's badge to Principal

Dandridge with my free hand. He wanted me to know that he thought it was a great shame that I was losing this honour, but student government had backed his decision and after bringing a 'violent date' to the dance he felt I no longer had the capabilities to use my better judgment, an essential trait for a prefect. The majority of student government was made up of Desmond and his supporters. I said nothing in defence of myself. There seemed to be no point and, it seemed, I had lost my voice from my terrible sore throat.

I moved through the rest of the school day like a silent and invisible being. Fellow students, who used to smile and call my name as I went by, looked right through me in the school halls as if I did not exist. No teacher called upon me to answer a single question in any of my classes, a fact of which I was glad since my voice was practically non-existent.

At lunch break, Janice came to find me on the rugby field where I sat amongst the pine needles alone. I had made the decision, as I traced my father's initials over and over again on the handkerchief, that completing the school year at Barnard High was no longer an option. There was a perfectly good all girls' public school, Parktown High, that was just as close to where we lived. My grades were all solid As and I hoped the fact that I had lost my status as a school prefect would be overlooked because of my strong academic record. I did not feel that leaving mid-term was a cowardly act, rather it was an act of acceptance. I no longer belonged at Barnard High. It was time for us to part company.

'Ruby.' Janice crunched heavily across the dried pine needles and stood in front of me. She twisted uncomfortably in her black patent-leather shoes and made no gesture to sit down. I watched her clasping and unclasping her pudgy hands as she spoke, 'Oh this is sooo hard for me.' She closed her eyes and took a deep breath as she blurted out what she needed to say. 'My mother said that it's not a good idea for me to be your friend any more. I'm unpopular enough.'

'It's okay,' I managed to get out in a raspy-thin voice but the effort to speak over inflamed tonsils made my throat ache even more.

'I'm so sorry.' She looked down at her feet. 'I really like you a lot, Ruby, but my mother . . .'

I held a hand up to stop her and smiled weakly up at her. She looked so painfully awkward and uneasy and I wanted to end this unpleasant task for her quickly.

'I understand,' I whispered, because my voice could offer up nothing more.

'Really?' She sounded pitifully relieved. She leaned down and suddenly kissed me on the cheek with a loud smack. 'Thanks for being such a pal!' She turned quickly and made a hasty exit. I thought back to Clive, who earlier had walked right past me with bobbing curls and down-cast eyes as we passed each other in the corridor between classes. I was somehow not surprised.

I opened and closed my fist round my father's handker-chief. It was the only thing that felt solid and real to me at Barnard High.

Pal. My mouth silently formed the word in my mouth. I was glad that Janice had said 'pal' and not 'friend' for that was all they both had ever been to me.

Chapter Twenty

Mother picked me up from school in her champagne-coloured Jaguar. She was bubbling over with exuberance and excitement about the list of attendees who would be coming to the exhibition and barely noticed how pale and quiet I was. I felt my skin shrinking like cling film, tighter and tighter round my legs, my arms, my torso. And a cold clamminess cloaked my body. When we pulled in through the gates Mother turned to look at me.

'Sorry, darling, I didn't even ask you how your day was.'

I shook my head.

'That bad. And your throat's killing you, right?'

I nodded.

She came to an abrupt stop outside the house. 'Right then, off to bed you go. I'll get some tea and honey up to you right away. I need you to be your usual perky self at the exhibition.'

I slept fitfully most of the afternoon in a haze of sweaty unease. It wasn't just the sore throat and throbbing head that kept waking me. There was something deeper that was churning in me, then seeping its way out through my pores. It was an uneasy sense of loss for something unnamed that I had yet to lose. I tried to force the dark feelings away with tender thoughts of Johann, but even those were laced with guilt. How could he want me when I had put him through hurt and humiliation already? Thoughts of Julian were no better. He too seemed to always suffer in my presence lately. And, as for school, there was no one who would come near me. I was treated like a diseased leper by everyone now. I was tainted by a sickness they could not see but did not want.

Father came up to check on me in the early hours of the evening. Mother must have come in and drawn the curtains when I was sleeping because my room was veiled in darkness. I knew it was Father by the faint, tired, lingering smell of his aftershave. He groped his way over and I felt the bed sag slightly from his weight as he sat down close to me.

'Ruby,' he whispered softly in the blackness that surrounded us. 'I've been thinking all day . . . maybe we should think about you leaving Barnard. There are other schools . . .'

I found his hand and squeezed it. He held on to mine tightly. 'These are such awful times.' He sighed. I clutched his hand even harder than I had held on to his handkerchief all day and felt a single tear slide down my damp cheek. 'Things will get better.' He patted the bedcovers as if to reassure me.

'When, Daddy?' I whispered in the darkness. 'When?'
'Soon. I promise.'

But I knew it was a promise that was not his to make.

Loretta called while I was propped up in bed eating a bowl of chicken broth, the only thing that felt good sliding past my swollen, raw tonsils.

'She can barely talk. Poor thing's got a nasty tonsillitis,' Mother informed her before she handed me the phone.

'Ruby, *ek is jammer dat jy siek is*, sorry for your illness . . .'

'Thanks,' I croaked.

'I will talk quickly then. Pa is very angry about what happened to Johann at your school dance. He is forbidding Johann and me to see you any more. But me and Johann, we talked and this is not going to be. I am your friend, *jou vriendin*, Ruby, no matter what anyone say . . .'

I gulped back tears but they came anyway.

'Johann says he will call you later . . . Pa is just getting home. *Totsiens* and feel better.' She hung up the phone quickly but I held the cradle against my heaving chest long after she had gone.

'Thank you,' I whispered into its small dark holes, which had carried the precious word I longed to hear.

'Friend'.

Chapter Twenty-One

I awoke the next morning with such excruciating razor-sharp pain in my throat that there was absolutely no possibility of attending school that day. Speaking was barely possible and I even had a hard time getting soothing lemon-flavoured tea and honey past my fist-like tonsils. There was something pleasantly calming about having lost my ability to speak. I could, for this brief voiceless time, live inside my own mind, undisturbed. It gave me the luxury to travel into nooks and crannies that I had long since overlooked, where I could stop and take out a forgotten thought or memory. I unpacked moments in my life, dusting some off and holding them out to be admired or unfurling one, only to roll it up quickly again. I lost track of time and even managed to stop feeling the sharp edges of my searing throat. I went through a myriad moments and memories, lingering with some, feeling their fabric soft and comforting and drawing quickly away from the rough-textured others. But there was one memory, although abrasive and harsh, I stayed with the longest.

*

*I am standing on the only shopping road in Parkview. I
am ten. I am waiting for my mother who is busy parking
her car. We are here to buy a new pair of party shoes
for me. There are lots of upcoming birthdays of girls in
my class. I am leaning against the wall outside the shoe
shop when a little girl with a pint-sized companion passes
by. He is black. They are holding hands. The late afternoon sun catches her wavy blonde hair and his dark,
tightly curled head. Suddenly a large woman walks
towards the small pair. She sees their hands clasped
together and shakes a big fat finger at them. Not allowed!
The little boy and girl stop dead in their tracks. Then the
large woman takes her chubby hands and separates
the little boy from the little girl so that their fingers are
no longer touching. I can see by their small little bodies
that they are afraid. The little girl hunches forward. The
little boy turns this way and that in little half-circles and
I get a quick glimpse of bewilderment on his small dark
face. What did I do wrong? Why is the lady angry? The
big woman, satisfied that she has accomplished what
needed to be done, moves on. She goes into the shoe
store that I am soon to be in with my mother. I can
smell her overpowering musky perfume as she strides by
me. I watch the small boy and girl walk away but they
are no longer holding hands. They probably won't ever
again. When my mother shows up a few minutes later I
tell her that I feel sick and don't want to buy shoes today.
'What do you feel, sweetheart?' she asks. Sad, I say. Sad
sick.*

*

A soft knock at the door comes just as I feel the gentle wind rush by me.

I am pedalling fast down a lush country road in Stellenbosch. Vineyards and pristine Cape Dutch houses blur by us. Mother is on a sky-blue bicycle beside me and I can see Father's legs pumping hard as he rides up ahead. I am eight and the sun is shining on this flawless day. We are having a wonderful two-week summer holiday in the Cape. Everything feels as sweet as the jasmine and morning glories that grow wildly on the side of the road. 'Catch me if you can, Mommy!' I stand up on the pedals and laugh and take off after my father. 'I'm on your tail, little bunny!' she shouts gleefully behind me . . .

Mother was at the door. She had a cup of something steaming hot on a tray for me.

'Drink this, darling. I just hung up with Dr Jacobs and he's sending over an antibiotic with the driver. He said he'll stop by later to take a look at you.' Mother plumped my pillows and touched my forehead. 'Cool as a cucumber. That's a good thing at least . . .'

While she coaxed me to take a sip of the clear chicken broth, I thought about how relaxed and enjoyable life had seemed when we were in the Cape, and how tense and complicated things had become now. I looked at Mother, the feathered lines round her mouth more pronounced, the furrowed line between her brows deeper, and wondered if she ever thought about those carefree times too.

'Your father and I talked about the whole school thing

last night. Let's get through the exhibition and this tonsil-litis first . . .'

She stayed in my room until I had forced every spoonful of broth down my raw throat. She chatted on about how much she liked Johann and how he reminded her of a boy she once dated when she was a student at Wits University. Big muscles with even bigger manners. When she mentioned Johann's name I felt a twinge of pleasure run up my spine. He had, as Loretta promised, called later that night and said that he would find a way to leave rugby practice early to come by and visit me the next day. The thought of Johann seeing me in this less-than-attractive sickly state was overshadowed by my longing to be with him again. Voice or no voice.

Before she left, Mother mentioned that Julian would be in the studio packing up all his paintings that needed to be hung for the exhibition, and she was sure he would be pleased to have a little company. 'If you feel up to it, meander down there, darling. He's understandably a little nervous. I'm off to the gallery now,' she said as she closed my bedroom door.

Although it had only been a few days since I last saw him, I missed Julian. His deep voice that never spoke a frivolous word, his quiet passion for things that mattered to him, but what I mostly missed was the time before things changed, when there was a natural ease between us. Still, I put on a pair of comfy corduroy trousers and an old sweater and made my way to the studio soon after I heard Mother's car engine start up.

*

I could hear the sound of popping bubble wrap as I opened the studio door. Julian was bent forward over a large frame, securing layer upon layer of the plastic protection around it.

He was so intent on his task that he did not hear the door open and with no voice to call his name, I went over to him and tapped him lightly on the shoulder. He was so startled that he let out a loud '*Hai!*' before turning round and seeing me there.

'I am jumpy like a rabbit!' He stood up and let out a sigh. 'And you are sick, from what your mother tells me.'

I pointed to my throat and nodded. I looked around the studio and saw that there were about a dozen paintings already wrapped and ready to go. They were stacked neatly against one wall but lying haphazardly on the floor and around the remaining studio walls were at least ten or more paintings still waiting to be bound. I made a gesture to Julian indicating that I wanted to help wrap the rest and hoped that he could make sense of my sign language.

He gave me a bemused smile. 'You can't speak . . . No voice,' he said, more as a statement than a question. I nodded. 'Wait!' He rushed over to a painting that was positioned on the ground and held it up for me to see. It was of a black woman in handcuffs. She was wearing her domestic nanny uniform. Blue starched apron, white cap over her short hair. A dark police truck was parked with its rear open. I could make out other servants, men and women alike, sitting on metal benches inside the truck. They were shackled to each other. A tall white policeman had his foot in the old nanny's back as he 'helped' her into the van. Her body was thrust forward in a stumbling motion.

'No voice?' Julian said excitedly. 'I have been thinking and thinking all morning what the name for this painting should be but nothing came and now you walk in and instantly it is there.' He quickly wrote on the back of its frame with a large marker: TITLE: *NO VOICE*.

I smiled and nodded, and he put his arm round me affectionately. 'You inspire me, Ruby. Did you know that?' He pointed with his free hand to another painting on the ground. 'You can help me wrap this one, if you like.'

I held the painting steady while Julian bound it with the cushiony protective plastic. It was an image of the township of Soweto from a distance but round its perimeter were a number of words written in bold child-like print. All of the words had been crossed out but were still legible. Only one word remained without a black line through it. It was the word SOuthWEsternTOwnships, which, if you chose just the capitalized letters, spelled SOWETO.

'There was a competition started in 1959 about what to call this newly formed township for blacks outside of Johannesburg. After four years of debating, the naming committee, which was all white, finally decided that it should be Soweto from those words, South Western Township, but there were many other names submitted.' Julian took the painting, now wrapped, and stacked it neatly against the wall along with the others. 'All of those were rejected because most of them were sent in by blacks

148

who actually lived in the township. Those are the words that are crossed out on my painting. You follow?'

I nodded.

'*Thari 'Ntshu*. The Black Nation. *Khethollo*. Segregation.' Julian came towards me with another painting in his hands that needed attention. 'And my favourite one that would never have been chosen, *Thinavhuyo*. It means, "We have nowhere to go."'

I wanted to tell him how much I liked the painting but all I could do was nod my head up and down enthusiastically.

'There was one Afrikaans name that they considered. It was the word *vergenoeg*. You know what it means, right?'

I reached for the black marker that Julian held and scribbled the translation on the top of my hand. 'Far enough'. And shrugged my shoulders as if to say, 'Why that?'

'Ah, Ruby, it means far enough away from us whites in Johannesburg. Far enough so that we will not be tainted by your blackness in any way. Far enough so that you can train or bus into the city of Johannesburg to work, but you will go far enough away to live so that we do not have to smell your food or hear your African languages being spoken or listen to your babies cry.'

I shook my head in disgust.

'*Vergenoeg*,' Julian said softly under his breath and sighed.

I wanted to tell Julian how brilliant I thought he was and how excited everyone was about the exhibition, but, instead, I chose to write something down that I thought he would want to know above all else. I found a notepad on the only table in the studio. It had various words and sketches on it and I flipped through to find a blank page. I scribbled quickly then handed Julian the piece of paper. He read it out aloud.

'*Father says that you are Mother's most talented artist. And I agree!*' Julian looked at the words a moment longer then folded the paper and put it carefully in his trouser pocket. 'Thank you, Ruby. That is very kind of your father and you. It means a great deal to me because you both mean a great deal to me. I will keep this note to remind me when I am in doubt about my purpose on this earth.'

We spent the remainder of the afternoon wrapping the rest of the paintings while Julian talked and explained his motivation and passion for each one. I heard Mother's car come through the driveway, followed by the sound of a second car right behind hers and assumed that Dashel was coming over to collect the wrapped works of art to take back to the gallery. While we were securing the last one, entitled *Despair is for the Defeated*, there was a knock at the studio door and Julian went to open it.

'Excuse me, but I am looking for Ruby. Her mother said she might be here.'

The voice was unmistakably Johann's.

'Yes, she is here,' Julian said quietly, and held the door open for Johann to enter.

I rose from my crouched position on the floor and watched as the two men took each other in. They were of even height, but Johann was far more beefy against

Julian's slighter frame. Johann looked confused, unsure who this tall black man was, dressed in khaki trousers and a button-down shirt who clearly was not a gardener or a domestic servant. I quickly went over and gave him a self-conscious hug before pointing from Julian to the wrapped paintings.

'I am an artist from Soweto,' Julian said slowly.

Johann nodded and held out his hand towards him, but Julian acted as if he hadn't noticed the gesture.

'I am Johann.' His hand remained frozen in mid-air before he withdrew it and put it affectionately round my waist.

I watched Julian's eyes travel then hold on Johann's fingers, which clasped my midsection. 'I know who you are.' His gaze remained fixed. 'But you, of course, did not know of me until this very moment. Am I correct?'

'*Ja*, Ruby has not mentioned . . .' Johann began, but Julian cut him off.

'Of course she hasn't. I am the invisible –'

I went to Julian's side and touched him on the arm and shook my head fervently. He flinched and pulled away from my touch.

'Yes, truth hurts.'

Johann stood unmoving, a look of bewilderment crossed his face. 'I should maybe leave . . . I did not know I was interrupting . . .'

A painful, strangled 'No!' came out of me, causing a stabbing sensation to knife through my throat. I moved towards Johann, then stopped. I was frozen between both of them and felt my legs grow thick and heavy as if cemented to the very floor. I looked from Johann to Julian and back again. Their eyes trained on me, waiting. But it was Johann who took a step towards me and reached for my hand.

'Come, you look ready to faint. We will get some air . . .'

I nodded helplessly and turned to Julian. His eyes were glazed over, as hard as two marbles. 'It's okay, Ruby. Go.'

'It was nice to meet you . . .' Johann said with polite civility.

'Julian. My name is Julian.' His voice came out harshly. 'Mambasa,' I heard him add as Johann closed the studio door behind us. I felt myself lift from the ground then fall, before the world went dark.

I could feel Johann's strong arms picking me up, but I must have floated in and out of consciousness as he carried me into the house and up the stairs with Mother's anxious voice filtering towards me. 'She's overburdened and exhausted,' I heard through the haze.

'She will be okay, Mrs Winters,' I heard Johann's deep, calm voice reply as if the words had been said in slow motion.

The sensation of warm small hands that pulled a blanket over me. Mother's tangerine smell hovered above.

A soft kiss on my temple from Johann's yielding lips and the smell of mint gum wafted over me.

In the space and time that I came and went, my mind present then missing, I heard Johann ask Mother about Julian then drifted out of consciousness just as her lilted voice lied that he caught the bus back to Soweto every night.

'Will Ruby Winters stand up? Will the real Ruby Winters please stand up and come on to the stage?' I cannot see the people in the audience, but I can hear loud applause that after a few seconds turns into angry booing. 'Roooooby Red, Rude be Red, Rude Ruby, Ruby Red! Ruby Red!' Then something cold hits me in the chest and I topple off the stage . . .

The ice-cold touch of Dr Jacobs' stethoscope against my skin woke me fully.

'Do you think you could stand, Ruby? Or maybe just sit up in bed? I need to listen to your lungs.'

It took me a few seconds to make sense of anything. It was dark outside and the lampshades in my bedroom had been lit. I sat up slowly while Dr Jacobs propped me forward. Mother was still there, pacing nervously back and forth. I looked around for Johann, but he was no longer in the room.

'I think she needs a tonic to boost her up. The problems she's having at school, losing her best friend and having an Afrikaans boyfriend is all much too stressful.'

I felt my cheeks grow hot at the mention of Johann as my boyfriend. It was not something that we had discussed.

Mother came to the bed and took my hand in hers. 'Johann sat by your bedside for at least two hours. Such a lovely boy. He had to get home for dinner. He was so worried about you . . .'

I felt a pool of disappointment fill me. I wanted to see him, touch him, be near him, but now he was gone.

'You've got to be well enough to come tomorrow night,' Mother said decisively as if her words could will good health back into me.

'Lungs are clear. I'm giving her an antibiotic shot as well as a cortisone one to reduce the swelling in her throat. Works like a charm.' Dr Jacobs reached into his black doctor's bag and took out two needles. I made a face at the sight of them. 'I know, Ruby, not fun, but it'll get you feeling better fast so you can make it to the exhibition. Or at least hobble there.'

As I felt the needle bite into my flesh, tears sprang to my eyes but it was from a pain far greater than its sharp point.

Chapter Twenty-Two

By 11.30 p.m. the gallery was already filled to capacity and the hum of many voices and clinking glasses was a cheering sound. Julian was sitting in the parking lot with Father in his heated Citroën and had been instructed not to enter until midnight. Mother liked to create a buzz, an excitement, a dramatic moment for the unveiling of a new artist. As such, she had each of Julian's paintings covered by red and black cloths that added to the theatrical spectacle. At the bewitching hour of midnight both the artist and his art would be undraped. Father always said that what made Mother's gallery so successful was her particularly original marketing flair. By the size of the crowd, she had done a superb job of getting influential art lovers, buyers and critics into her renowned gallery. There was a smattering of blacks amongst the well-heeled whites. I could not help noticing a regal African woman in traditional headdress and colourful garb as she stood next to her husband who wore an ill-fitting black suit. I knew him to be a member of the underground African National Congress who Father had helped to get out of jail. He and his wife had eaten dinner in our home about a year ago after his release and I had marvelled at her beautiful beaded bracelets. There were at least half a dozen or so other black men and women who looked familiar to me. They too were other members of the ANC. I recognized them from underground meetings that used to be held at our house a few years ago before things got too dangerous and Mother and Father made the decision to close our large iron gates to the outside world for the most part. I looked nervously around the room for the sight of a dark crew cut on the head of a grey-eyed man, the undercover cop who had wanted me to warn my mother. I breathed a sigh of relief when I did not see his large unpleasant form lurking about the gallery.

Dr Jacobs' magic injection had certainly improved my condition. My throat was far less swollen and hurt only a little. This drastic improvement gave me back my voice, something I was not sure I even wanted. I had taken Mother's advice and had not gone to school that day. It did not require her twisting my arm very much at all since Barnard High was the last place I wanted to be. Instead, I had spent the morning with Julian, helping him choose the black trousers and open-necked maroon dress shirt that he would wear for the exhibition. He did not mention his encounter with Johann the day before and I was glad that we were able to focus instead on the much-anticipated night ahead. He had not been aware of my fainting spell until Mother had told him to watch out that I didn't 'keel over' before she left for the gallery.

Julian had kept checking, every few minutes or so, to see

if I was feeling okay and whether I needed water to drink. I was touched, as I always was, by his deep concern for me.

Father had made sure that I'd eaten dinner and taken all my medicines before dropping me off at the gallery at 10 p.m. I wore a black polo neck and slim-fitting black trousers to match Dashel and Thandi. It was the 'staff uniform' whenever we had events. Mother usually wore something colourful in silk.

As Thandi and I stood shoulder to shoulder in the gallery kitchen, preparing the 'fake trays' of wine and champagne that would be stacked in the back, should we need them, Dashel breezed in to check on us.

'Girls, girls, girls, it's a full house tonight!' He grabbed a glass of champagne out of Thandi's hands and gulped it down with a flourish. 'I am parched! Talked the ear off the art critic from the *London Times*. Girls, did you hear that? The *London Times*! Your mother is a genius . . .' He kissed me on the top of my head and breezed out again.

'*Yirra*, but this is quite a turnout!' Thandi wiped the perspiration from above her upper lip. 'It's gonna be a *morse* big night!' She swivelled her hips and placed the finished tray carefully with the others.

'Yes,' I croaked, 'it is.'

When we had finished the tray task, I laced my way through the crowd to the brightest spot in the room. Mother was wearing a lavender silk skirt with canary-yellow mules and a matching yellow ruffled shirt. She had a beautiful lavender-and-gold silk scarf tied in a large bow in her hair, and her dangling gold earrings swayed like miniature chandeliers as she talked enthusiastically to a group of people who had gathered around.

'No, I haven't been hiding him as some clever ploy,' she laughed. 'I've been keeping him safe. And now you're all about to meet him.' She raised the fluted stem in her hand and clinked glasses with the eager group, 'To the unveiling of Julian!' she said. It was followed by a collective murmur of agreement.

'Ruby, darling!' she said as she saw me. 'Feeling okay? Be a love and tell Thandi to go to the car and bring Julian in through the kitchen. Have him wait there until I give the okay. And have her tell your father to come in; I'm about to make a speech.'

Midnight is the celebrity hour of the day. It is the designated time when magic things happen, when time takes on a special mysterious aura. It is also an unforgiving and unyielding time. It is the moment when one day steals away and another shimmers in, where the mistakes we made in the past twenty-four hours cannot be changed or erased and the joys and pleasure that we experienced cannot be relived. We now refer back to that time as 'yesterday'. It becomes a part of our history, a place we cannot return to or alter ever again except in our minds. It heralds the delivery of a new beginning and the passing of something old. It was for me, and all that were there that night, a midnight never to forget.

Mother began speaking just a few minutes before the appointed hour. Being small, she had positioned herself on top of a chair so that everyone could see her. Dashel stood holding its flimsy arm steady on one side while Father, who had brought Julian in through the back door and into the kitchen, and left him there alone to wait for his cue, stood on the other side.

Julian's paintings remained covered by their red-and-black cloths, which would be removed by 'the gallery staff' when Mother said the word after Julian had been brought out and introduced.

The crowd spilled out of the Gallery Grande and into the smaller galleries and people strained to see Mother over the tops of too many heads. There was a gentle clinking of glasses, a settling of feet and someone coughed, but for the most part a hush fell over the room as Mother began to speak.

'Good morning, everyone!' There was a general titter. 'I think I can say that, since it's the beginning of a new day . . . my watch says twelve-oh-one.' Mother held her naked wrist up and pretended to look at an imaginary watch. More titters followed. 'This is also the beginning of a new era in township art and the voice of black artists in a country of oppression.' She raised her manicured hand as soft applause broke out amongst some in the crowd. My throat started to ache again and a light-headedness came over me. I wished I could have had Johann's strong arm round my waist to hold me up but Mother and Father had agreed that it was out of the question to invite him. I knew they were right. Apart from the obvious reasons, this was Julian's night and I did not want to let anything ruin it for him. I placed my hand instead on the wall beside one of Julian's covered works to steady myself and tried to concentrate on Mother's next words.

'Ernest Hemingway, in *A Farewell to Arms,* wrote about a character named Frederic Henry who is put to the test during the madness and atrocity of World War One.' Mother raised her voice an octave. 'He was a man of action, self discipline, but, most importantly, he was a man who was able to maintain "grace under pressure".' She paused for dramatic effect and held her hand in the direction of the closed kitchen door, which was to her left. 'Ladies and gentleman, Julian Mambasa is such a man. He has sustained his focus, his passion, his discipline and most of all his gentle grace, under extreme conditions and under intense pressure. He is an extraordinary artist, as you will soon see, but, most importantly, he is a remarkable human being who is able to take the pain and suffering of the human condition of his time and his people and share it with us through his work.' Mother's voice crackled with emotion. 'I am honoured, and humbled and proud to introduce you to . . . Julian Mambasa!'

As she said his name I felt the world tilt at an unnatural angle and my stomach lurched as the crowd applauded loudly and enthusiastically. Dashel moved to the kitchen door and flung it open in a majestic flourish. All eyes in the room, including mine, were riveted to the door. The door that would bring forth Julian, the new young face of African art, the carrier of the torch of his people. The applause got louder and then suddenly stopped. A terrifying void, where hands that were just seconds before pounding together with excitement now covered their mouths. I do not know if I first heard the shocked gasp or first saw the face of the man I so feared inside the kitchen door under its frame. It was the searing cold grey eyes and dark crew-cut head of the undercover detective that faced us all. He raised his gun as the crowd moaned collectively; someone screamed and in the sudden chaos the frightened patrons tried to disperse.

'Everybody freeze! Nobody move!' the detective yelled in a harsh guttural voice.

I had been unable to move anyway. I had risen above the gallery momentarily, not wanting to stay on the cruel ground below. I watched my mother topple and fall from the chair, her skirt billowing upwards as someone knocked her down in their panic to escape. She lay, small and crumpled, the lavender skirt and yellow blouse her only shield against the onslaught of blue-uniformed policemen who now entered the gallery from all sides, guns raised, their voices bellowing commands to us in both English and Afrikaans. We did what most people do in the face of loaded guns. We raised our hands.

I was close against the wall and while my one hand was raised, I propped the other protectively against the wall next to one of Julian's covered paintings. I looked into Father's face across the room. I knew his eyes had been furtively seeking mine as soon as the police burst through the doors. When he found me in the crowd a look of relief flooded his face followed by a look of unmistakable anger. I held his gaze. It gave me the strength to do what I did next. I slowly inched my hand forward and let my fingers grasp the tiniest edge of the black-and-red cloth that covered Julian's painting. I did not move another muscle but kept my eyes trained on my father's face as I slowly pulled the cloth away and let it fall to the ground. I dared not turn to look and see which painting I had exposed, but I knew by the small triumphant smile on Father's lips that it was an important one.

'Not such a clever girl after all.' The looming form of the plain-clothes detective approached me. 'I told you to warn your mother.' He grabbed my wrist, yanked it off the wall and twisted it. 'And all for this . . .' he sneered, and looked at the painting that I had bared for all to see. It was the last one that we had wrapped. *Despair is not for the Defeated*.

He spat at the picture frame. 'A *kaffir* whore carrying too many loads of laundry on her head! Bleddy stupid if you asks me.' He sniffed the air like he did the first time he'd been in the gallery as if he could smell the tired middle-aged woman's sweat. He gave my wrist a hard squeeze before releasing it and I tried not to let even the smallest sound escape my mouth.

It was Father who made the next move. Perhaps he was spurred on by my small act of defiance or by the detective's harsh treatment of me or, perhaps, as an attorney, who had dealt with the law on a regular basis, he knew what came next. With his hands still in the air Father shouted across the silent and terrified crowd now surrounded by policemen. He aimed his words at the detective, who was approaching the beautiful black woman in her colourful traditional clothes.

'I am a lawyer. I have the right to ask where my client, Mr Mambasa is. I would like an answer.' Father baited him, as if to draw him away from the petrified woman and her political-activist husband, who stood stoically beside her.

'I knows who you are, Mr Winters. Yes, we at the Special Branch have a very thick file on you. ANC supporter, Rivonia Trial lawyer, defender of the natives.' The detective took a cigarette out of his chequered jacket pocket and lit it. He spoke through the smoke rings that spun one after another into the face of the beautiful black woman like barbed wire coils. 'You are, Mr Winters, what we call a *kaffir-boetie*, a black-lover who will risk his own hide for these vermin.' He took a step towards the regal woman and blew a stream of smoke straight into her nostrils. I watched her husband clench his fists, which were still raised above his head. The woman began to cough uncontrollably.

The detective laughed. 'Couldn't handle all that up your big nostrils? I'm sure you've had other things pumped up there!'

'Enough!' It was Mother's voice that echoed across the gallery causing the detective to stop his assault and turn in her direction.

Mother was surrounded by three young policemen with matching bad crew cuts. She had pulled herself up to a standing position and was the only one in the room without her hands above her head. Those small delicate hands now pointed a finger slowly and methodically around the room at various patrons. 'Mr Matheson from the *London Times*, you can put your hands down.' The nervous moustached gentleman tentatively did as she instructed. 'Mr Bates of the *San Francisco Chronicle* –' her finger trained on him – 'please feel free to do the same.' She searched the room for another face. 'Miss Williamson, is it?' The young redheaded woman nodded nervously. 'Brand-new art critic from our very own *Rand Daily Mail* –' Mother said the words carefully as if to make a point – 'please lower your hands.' The young woman eyed a gun that was drawn close to her but hesitantly did the same.

I could feel the shift in the room as the policemen seemed suddenly restless, their guns not quite as steady, their legs shifting from one to the other as Mother went around the room and asked people, one by one, to lower their hands.

The steel-eyed detective ground his cigarette out on the smooth gallery floor and looked from one reporter to another. He clearly had not realized there had been that much media present. It would never have occurred to him that important newspapers would care about a black man from Soweto's art. I had learned over the years from being the daughter of political parents that there was nothing that a government who ran their country on fear and torture hated more than press, especially foreign press. South Africa presented its gold and diamonds to glitter in the face of other nations and hid their unjust oppression and brutality under censorship and laws.

I watched curiously as the detective suddenly made the signal for his men to lower their weapons. It was as if the bullets aimed at the crowd held no power any more.

'Now if you would be kind enough to answer my husband,' my mother said firmly, 'where is Mr Mambasa?'

'Arrested.' He smirked. An audible gasp went out amongst the crowd. 'Didn't have his passbook on him when I –'

'When you lay in wait outside the gallery and ambushed

him once he was alone.' Mother moved towards the detective. 'And you are . . .? Take note,' she said as she passed the journalist from the *San Francisco Chronicle*. The reporter now appeared far less afraid and reached for the pen and pad in his breast jacket pocket and began writing.

'I am Detective Groenewald. Member of the Special Forces,' he said, looking at the reporter. 'Does the yankee need me to spell it?'

The reporter shook his head quickly.

'Where is my client now?' Father walked towards the detective and joined Mother. I wanted to go and throw my arms round them both and sob or laugh, but I stood still, with one hand close to Julian's beloved painting. What Detective Groenewald had missed in the work of art was that, if you looked closely, the tired washerwoman was walking on the camouflaged faces of angels that stared up at you from the dusty, potholed path. The old woman's raw knobbled feet stepped on their compassionate, loving faces as they tried to soften each aching step that she took.

It did not surprise me that Detective Groenewald had not noticed them. He would never have thought to look for angels on a dusty street in Soweto.

In the end, the night of Julian's exhibition turned out to be a night of triumph. Detective Groenewald and his men tried to make a bullish show by demanding the passbooks of all the other black people in the room, who luckily all had the right papers with them. He left angrily, but without making a single arrest, including Julian, who was being held in a police van in the parking lot until Mother, never one to overlook all unpleasant possibilities, produced Julian's sacred passbook that she had put in her bag for safekeeping. His passbook gave him permission to be in Johannesburg and in Sandton, which was where the gallery was. Mother had made sure of that fact. Detective Groenewald and his men even stood by and watched as Dashel, Thandi and I quickly passed out the fake trays to the black patrons, who immediately began acting as hired serving people. There was nothing illegal about that, Mother pointed out to him. She made it very clear to the detective that she had asked the black helpers to put their trays in the kitchen before her speech began. She wanted everyone's undivided attention. He could not argue with that.

After Julian was unshackled and released from the police van he walked into the gallery through the kitchen door to a thunderous applause that lasted for many minutes. We happily removed all the red-and-black cloths and at last everyone was able to see the depth and brilliance of his work.

Over the next few weeks, in the newspapers in Johannesburg and London and San Francisco, it was said that a star had been set free and now held his place in the heavens. 'BLACK ARTIST'S ARREST AT EXHIBITION OPENING IS THWARTED' made Julian, and Mother's gallery, instantly famous in the art community around the word.

Even Mother, with her original and innovative marketing skills, could not have come up with such an effective launch plan.

Chapter Twenty-Three

The mood in our house went from one of tension and anxiety to one of relaxed chaos. The telephone did not stop ringing both at home and at the gallery with requests for interviews with Mother and Julian from art critics and newspapers local and abroad. A steady stream of people came to the gallery every day to see Julian's works, and Dashel joked that we should start charging an entrance fee at the door.

Most of Julian's paintings were bought rather quickly and had orange stickers marking SOLD on each one. They would go to their new owners once the exhibition was over in a month. Julian seemed quietly baffled by all the attention he was now getting but Mother kept telling him, 'I told you so.'

Fame, it seemed, had a unique way of instilling a false sense of safety into our world. Mother and Father behaved as if a shield had suddenly been placed on our house, guarding against any ills that might befall us. It was as if Glorious Attention was an armour-suited knight whose silver sword was all encompassing. As such, for a brief period, Mother and Father seemed to overlook the fact that we were still under surveillance and our doors were once again opened to ANC members who came and went in the still, dark hours of the night.

With the exhibition opening behind him and now having established himself in the art community, Julian began to direct his energy towards his hatred of the government's system of apartheid. In the weeks that followed, he spent less time in the gallery and more time in Father's office in closed-door meetings with other black men and women. Julian would sleep most of the day because he was up a good deal of the night now. His bedroom door was usually still closed as I passed by when I returned from school in the afternoons. The only time, it seemed, that Julian altered his daytime sleeping routine was if there were an interview arranged. Mother would rouse him, then drive him to the gallery where the meetings would take place. Julian, always uncomfortable with scrutiny, let her do most of the talking. He answered questions directed at him in short, clipped sentences. Although not his inten-tion, he was often written about as a brooding, angry young artist whose pain and fury were as prevalent in his art as they were in his persona. This, of course, evoked even greater intrigue and drew more curious reporters to him.

One afternoon, after a particularly miserable day at school, I rode to the gallery and sat in on an interview in Mother's office that had just begun. It soon became clear to me why Julian was getting such a reputation.

'Mr Mambasa, can you tell us what inspired you to

become an artist?' the eager young journalist in a pin-striped suit and thinning hair asked, pen poised.

'*Harold and the Purple Crayon*,' Julian said, without missing a beat.

A look of confusion crossed the novice journalist's face. 'I'm sorry, can you explain what that is . . .?'

But Julian, satisfied that he had answered the question, gave the young man a blank stare. Mother, realizing that Julian had said all he wanted on the subject, chimed in quickly to embellish.

'*Harold and the Purple Crayon* is a wonderful children's book that Julian first heard when he was just a small boy. His mother was a domestic servant and the madam of the house was reading the book to her son. Julian, who was supposed to be in the kitchen helping out, hid behind the living-room door and listened to the whole story. It seemed to resound in his young soul.'

'I see . . .' The young journalist wrote haltingly. 'And what is it about?'

Mother was suddenly at a loss for words, clearly unable to remember the details of the story. She glanced over at Julian for assistance but his eyes were focused on a spot on the floor.

'It's about the ability to draw your way out of your problems. And create a solution,' I said quickly.

Julian, who had been fiddling with a loose thread on his faded denim shirt, looked up at me and nodded slowly. Our eyes locked and I knew that he was pleased with my response. He gave the journalist a few more platitudes and then let Mother handle the rest of the questions. But, when the young man asked Julian what colour he liked best to paint in, a look of disgust crossed his face. He stood up and left the room, indicating that the interview was over, leaving Mother to offer a profuse apology and a glass of fine port that she kept for special occasions.

'There is nothing more desirable than a bad boy,' Dashel said, after I told him about the interview and had collapsed into a chair in his office.

'He's not a bad boy, Uncle D,' I murmured as I lay back on the soft black leather and closed my eyes. 'Desmond and his nasty group are bad boys and they're hardly desirable.'

I was feeling horribly tired and my head ached from trying to keep myself sane and calm at Barnard High until the term was over, which was not for three more weeks. Everyone at school knew that I would be leaving then to go to Parktown Girls' High. Gossip spread faster than weeds and it wasn't long after the faculty had been informed by Principal Dandridge that Ruby Winters, ex-prefect and ex-popular girl, would be taking permanent leave of their beloved educational institution that all the students knew of my imminent departure too.

The rumour circulating was that I was leaving to join Johann at Steunmekaar and many snide remarks were made behind my back, but loud enough for me to hear, to that effect. But, to my surprise, there were a few students who let me know surreptitiously that they were sorry to see me leave. The boys who still cared patted me on the back quickly as I passed them in the school corridors and a few of the braver girls even dropped notes on my desk that said things like, 'We'll think of you often,' or, 'So sad that you're leaving but it's probably for the best. Good luck!' I was still *persona non grata* to everyone in our matric class so I started spending lunch break in the library as the weather was bitterly cold. I began reading Hemingway's *A Farewell to Arms* since Mother had quoted it in the speech that she had made about Julian. The words 'grace under pressure' had resonated inside me when she'd spoken them, and it became a silent incantation that I said to myself to help me get through the day at school. Grace in the face of disgrace, as it were.

Had it not been for my late-night calls with Loretta, who would call after her *pa* was asleep, and then Johann, who would take the phone from his sister when we were done having girl-chat, I do not know how I would have endured my last weeks at Barnard High. Loretta and Johann were my only true friends now, despite the fact that we lived miles apart.

'No worries, Ruby. You will be happier at your new school.' Loretta would try to make me feel better when I told her of the loneliness and isolation I felt.

'I dread every day. I wish I could be at school with you,' I told her many times.

'*Ja, ek ook*. But you learn in English and me in Afrikaans. It is language that separates people, isn't it? Not only religion.'

'Yes,' I said, thinking that Johann and Loretta spoke 'the language of the government' and they were judged on that fact by Julian and other blacks, just as Julian and his people were judged by their skin colour. I would be judged differently too by a certain group of people in a few weeks when they saw me in a state-school uniform and not a private one. It all seemed so unfair. We didn't get a chance to be accepted or rejected by who we were as individuals, rather it was our outside packaging that determined everything. Language, skin colour and even uniform.

'Don't be sad.' Loretta must have heard the deflated sound in my voice. '*Alles moet verby gaan.* Do you know what that means?'

'I think so . . .' I said.

'It means "everything must pass".'

'I just wish these last few weeks at Barnard would pass quickly.' I sighed.

'They will. I will tell them to!' she said sweetly. And we both laughed.

Because their father had forbidden them from seeing me, I could no longer go over to visit Loretta in her home, and skipping after-school activities was difficult for her. However, Johann, having a car and far more freedom, was able to escape his father's scrutiny and managed to meet me as often as he could. He would sometimes ditch rugby practice and sneak away in the late afternoons. Our rendezvous spot was always Zoo Lake in Saxonwold. It was a quick bike ride down Westcliff Ridge and a short distance on Jan Smuts Avenue for me before I was in his arms.

I rode, not caring about cars and traffic and possible

surveillance, with my legs pumping as fast as my heart in his direction. Johann would usually be waiting in the small cafe that was close to the lake's edge. There, we would share a sundae or sometimes even rent a rowing boat and go out on the icy water. It was winter and the lake was almost always deserted and I would watch his strong arms row, his eyes never leaving mine as he faced me, with the watery afternoon sun closing like a pale gold halo behind him.

When we reached the furthest side of the lake, and Johann had pulled the boat into a secluded enclave where the weeping willow trees formed a soft green curtain around us, we would reach for each other, our mouths melting together, our hands tracing rapid paths on each other's skin as if we were writing rushed, tender words that could be read long after we were apart. There was an urgency in us both to hold on and not let go. Our unspoken thoughts translated in body code that our time together was precious and that the only thing that mattered was now.

I cannot say how many times Johann and I met, perhaps a dozen or so, I don't know, but I do remember with aching clarity that the last time we held each other was at Zoo Lake. It was a Tuesday afternoon. Sometimes I can still hear the water lapping softly, as if kissing our rowing boat, somehow knowing that young lovers were entwined above, supported in its liquid arms.

'I miss you before we are even apart.' Johann stroked my hair and pulled me close before reaching for the oars that would take us back to the shore.

'I miss you always,' I said, and ran my fingers up and down the inside of his forearm where the skin was smooth. He took my hand and held it to his lips. 'You are my one and only,' he said, before releasing it.

There was a family of ducks that swam beside us as Johann rowed steadily through the water. The sun was setting fast now and the light over the bank made the land look mottled in shades of violet and brown. The sight of the dock ahead filled me with a murky sense of something that I could not define and a cold shiver ran up my spine. I looked at Johann whose strong body encased the softest of hearts and was filled with a sudden wave of panic. I did not want us to dock; I wanted Johann and I to float on the placid water forever, away from dry land where dark things like school principals, detectives and angry Afrikaans fathers lurked in shadowy places, where police watched with accusing eyes and school friends disappeared in the blink of an eye.

The mother duck suddenly quacked loudly, as if to warn her brood that danger might be lurking, and they all turned and followed her in a direction away from our boat.

'I'm scared,' I said.

'Don't be. I'll always keep you safe.'

We kissed quickly on the shore and I got on my bike and pedalled home fast before darkness fell. Had I known what lay ahead I would have clung to Johann and made him promise that we would be together forever.

But, of course, I didn't.

Chapter Twenty-Four

Wednesday, 16 June 1976. The day that changed my life. The day that changed the lives of thousands of people, forever.

It began like any other school day. It was the morning after Johann and I had met at Zoo Lake. It began as they all did. Throwing on my school uniform, wolfing down a buttered piece of toast followed by a gulp of coffee, then jumping on to my bike with my book satchel on my back.

I rode fast in the freezing morning air down the hill with my woolly scarf blowing behind me and my gloved hands gripping the handlebars, teeth chattering with each icy blast of air that knifed through me. I reached school in record time, wanting to escape the chilly winds as quickly as I could.

There was the all too familiar hollowness in the pit of my stomach as I parked my bike and made my way to my first class, which was biology. The school bell rang at 7.30 a.m. just as we opened our textbooks to the chapter on the pulmonary system. What I did not know until later that day was that while we sat in our heated classrooms there was another group of young students many miles away from us who were far from warm and safe in their classrooms. They stood on the potholed streets, their shivering fingers wrapped round homemade signs that read, 'Down With Afrikaans', 'Viva Azania!' and 'If we must do Afrikaans then Prime Minister Voster must do Zulu.' Bracing themselves against the cold morning air, these students had begun gathering at the Thomas Motolo Junior Secondary School in a suburb of Soweto. It appeared in the papers the next day that most of them had arrived at school with no knowledge that the Soweto Student's Representative Council had decided that today would be a day of peaceful demonstration against the impending law that would force all black children to learn their subjects in Afrikaans. The students eagerly joined the march.

While we were learning that *Tyrannosaurus rex* and a modern sparrow had something in common – an almost identical pulmonary system – the protesting youth of the township had grown to several thousand as they marched through the streets of Soweto, gathering students from Naledi High School, Malopo Junior and others. They sang the African national anthem, '*Nkosi Sikelel' iAfrika*', and hung crudely made signs on their deserted schools that said, 'No Security Branch Police allowed. Enter at your own risk.'

While we made our way to the next period, holding our glossy textbooks in our fair-skinned hands, the marching students were joined by thousands more from Meadowlands, Diepkloof and other schools. They all converged on Vilakazi Street outside Orlando West High and Phefeni Junior.

While I began my English Literature essay, 'Is untimely death an act of fate or divine intervention?', that was based on our prescribed book, *The Bridge of San Luis Rey* by Thornton Wilder, the animated crowd of black students, standing shoulder to shoulder, blocked Vilakazi Street. They chanted in harmony, their voices as one, 'Power! Power!' as more students kept joining the throng of thousands.

It was then that the police made their presence felt.

The white officers, dressed in their blue uniforms, lined up side by side down the centre of the road. They stood less than twenty feet from the children. Then more policemen came and, followed by the riot squad police with snarling dogs and weapons, they descended from their oversized police trucks.

I wrote my essay rapidly, my hand tearing across the page: 'This book, which covers the aftermath of an inexplicable tragedy, where a small footbridge in Peru breaks and sends five people to their deaths, lets us examine whether these innocent people were meant to die or if they fell to their deaths randomly. Why those five? Could it have been them or anyone else?'

It was later reported that a woman, with a baby tied to her back in a soft Sotho blanket, asked one of the policemen as he cocked his rifle, 'Are you going to kill our children?' But he told her no. There would be no killing. As his words left his lips, tear gas was hurled by one of his fellow officers into the crowd of young students who tried to retaliate with rocks and stones. Shots, one after the other, were fired into the unarmed youths. *Bang! Bang! Bang!* Why those two? Why those five? Why those fourteen?

I was pleased with the essay I had written. I felt that I had given a fair argument and explanation to the second paragraph of the essay question: 'To the gods are we perhaps like flies that are killed by boys on a summer's day or has every feather that falls from even the smallest bird been brushed gently away by the hand of God?'

Screaming children tried to disperse. Chaos, cries for help, more shots fired into the crowd. Seventeen-year-old Antoinette Peterson searched in vain for her little brother, Hector. She saw a group of youths surrounding a small boy who lay bleeding on the ground. Later I learned, with the rest of the world, that Hector was the first child shot down by the police. Twelve and in grade six. He would never see grade seven. An image shown all over the newspapers. It is seared in my mind. Hector, carried by a lanky boy in tattered overalls, his sister, Antoinette, a look of horror on her face, runs beside his lifeless body as they head towards the clinic in vain. More images that came later . . . Children carrying wounded children out of the tear gas. Smoke, then fire as the angry mob begins to torch cars, houses, stores. 'Tear Soweto down. It is a symbol of our oppressors!'

*

An announcement was made on the intercom system right before the end of last period. It was Principal Dandridge.

'Students, it has been reported on the radio that unruly blacks in Soweto have started rioting. There is nothing for you to be alarmed about. It doesn't affect any of you. The township is miles from here but as a precaution we ask that you all travel home with a friend and not alone. Thank you.'

I stood, moments later, with the rest of the class as the last bell of the day rang.

Not affected. Not affected, echoed in my brain. *I fear there will be bloodshed.* Father's words rolled slowly towards me as I grabbed my satchel and moved in slow motion into the corridor.

'Buncha natives causing trouble,' I heard behind me.

'Throw them some bananas. That'll stop 'em!' another joked as they all laughed.

I pushed through the throng, willing my leaden feet to go faster and faster as I raced out of the building. There was only one word pounding through my brain, pushing me to fly at lightning speed through the school gates and up the first hill. Faster. Faster. Faster! One force, one thought, one focus.

Eyes of liquid pools, arms of strength and comfort, hands that created magic.

Julian!

Chapter Twenty-Five

I raced up the stairs to Julian's bedroom and flung the door open, hoping that he was still sleeping and did not yet know about the riots, but all that greeted me was a bundle of lumpy bed sheets. I prayed that I would find him in the studio, but it was Mother who stood in the middle of the empty room. She turned as I threw the door open. A look of disappointment crossed her face when she saw that it was me and not Julian standing in the doorway. Her eyes were filled with sunken distress.

'He's gone,' she said quietly.

'No!'

'I left the gallery as soon as word reached me that there were killings in Soweto. But too late . . .' Her voice wavered.

I ran to her and we held each other, breathing in the paint fumes and his musky scent, the air thick with the memory of his every bold stroke and charcoaled sketch mark.

'He left a note.' She released me and held out a shaking hand. I took the crumpled piece of paper from her and opened it.

My wonderful family, I can no longer remain in the safety of your world. It is time for me to rejoin my people in Soweto and fight for our freedom. I know you will understand.

Julian

I felt my heart wrench and tear away from its mooring in my chest. 'We'll never see him again, Mother!' I cried.

She took my hands in hers as tears streamed down her face. 'My darling child, he is a warrior. A fighter. A survivor.'

'No! He is an artist.'

She gripped my fingers even tighter as I angrily tried to release them.

'Ruby, listen to me. We had him on borrowed time. I knew that. He is a soldier whose weapon until now has been a paintbrush. I have always believed in its power but it will take weapons of another kind to bring about change.' She released my hands. 'Now we must set him free to do what his soul has yearned for since he was a boy.'

'What is that, Mother?' My tearstained face looked anxiously into hers for an answer.

'To use his purple crayon. Whether it takes the form of . . . a paintbrush or a gun.'

'He's a member of the ANC, isn't he, Mother?'

'Yes,' she said haltingly. 'He is an artist and an activist. He has the ability to do what few can.' Her voice was barely audible. 'He can open people's eyes but also close them.'

'I don't understand . . .?'

'Kill, Ruby.' She struggled to get the words out. 'He will, if he must. For his people's sake.'

Mother and I sat glued to the radio for the rest of the day. She got up only to answer the kitchen phone and we would give each other a hopeful look every time it rang. Julian? But each time she returned to the living room, shaking her head. Reports were coming in on SABC radio that police vans had been set on fire as well as administration offices in Soweto. There were rumblings that the rioting would spread the next day throughout other townships. What was not reported, but that we later learned, was that the Special Branch had begun a widespread crackdown on ANC members and supporters and that white sympathizers were being put under house arrest or worse.

Father came home by nightfall and found Mother and I sitting forlornly in the living room with cups of cold untouched tea on the table in front of us.

'My lovely ladies.' He opened his arms to us and we went into them like two lost kittens.

'I would have expected nothing less from Julian,' Father said stoically. 'Come, Annabel, we have lots to do. The forces are moving fast.' He gave her a knowing look.

'Will you be all right, darling?' Mother asked.

I nodded.

'Won't be long.' Father kissed me on the top of my head. I watched as Mother followed him dutifully to his office and heard the door smack shut behind them.

I wandered upstairs and lay on my bed, my eyes pulled

into Julian's painting, the purple crayon in the boy's hand. *Where are you, Julian?* I asked the image. *Where are you?* Outside my bay window I heard the unseasonal cry of a piet-my-vrou bird trill a warning that the rains would be coming. But it was winter and the rains would not fall for many months. I wondered if the little bird was trying to send me a warning of another kind or if it were confused, perhaps, like everyone else today since our world had been turned dangerously upside down.

I phoned Loretta and she sounded strange and distant. I asked her what was wrong and she whispered into the phone that her *pa* had come home early on account of the riots and that he was cross-questioning their servant at the moment. She hung up quickly and I didn't even have a chance to ask when Johann might be home.

A sudden loud thud on my window made me sit up with a start. I went over and opened it, the scent of lavender and fresh mint that grew below wafting up at me. I squinted into the darkness. There below stood the familiar shape of the person I so longed to see.

'Julian!'

'Shhh!' he whispered back. 'Come quickly. Say nothing.'

I quickly put on a pair of shoes and a coat and hurried down the stairs, my heart beating fast as I walked past the still-closed study door. When I reached the garden outside my bedroom Julian was no longer there. I looked around furtively with a sinking feeling in my chest, then I heard a rustling in the bushes.

'Here,' came Julian's voice from behind the shrubbery. In the dim shadows I gingerly made my way to him.

'Give me your hand, Ruby,' he said softly.

I held it out across the open space between us then felt his fingers warm and yielding in my palm. He pulled me down towards him and crushed me hard against his chest. I could smell the flames of Soweto on his coat.

'I went in and it is bad. Children have been killed – did you know?'

'The news isn't saying much about casualties.'

'I stood amongst the injured and the dead and do you know what I thought about?'

'No,' I whispered back.

'You.' He hugged me even tighter as if he were inhaling my very essence before he released me gently.

'I came back to take in your sweet spirit, your goodness, Ruby. To bottle it inside me so that I can draw on it for strength when I am far from you because there may never be another time.'

'Don't leave!' I pleaded, gripping the lapels of his coat.

'I must. It was not easy getting in or out, but I have friends on the inside. The police have sealed Soweto. They are cutting off food supplies tomorrow.'

'Julian, the Special Branch . . . they're arresting all known ANC members.'

'Yes, I know. Tell your mother, the ANC, they are sending me underground to Mozambique for special training.' Julian pulled me to my trembling feet. 'Tell your father that I was wrong. My people *are* ready for change.'

He brusquely turned me to face him. 'Know that wherever you are, I am with you.'

'Julian, please!' I held on to his jacket but he gently unclenched my fingers and held my icy fingers to his lips.

'Goodbye, Ruby.'

He turned quickly before I had a chance to protest again. Through lavender-and-mint tears, I strained to watch him as he walked away, but the darkness swallowed him up all too quickly.

Chapter Twenty-Six

School the next day was unbearable for me. Our safe world was only interrupted once by the Soweto Riots in the form of the announcement the day before by Principal Dandridge to leave school property with a friend. But, today, everything at Barnard High was business as usual with not a single mention of any killings or massive protests in our very city.

As expected, the students in other townships followed in the wake of the Soweto students and there was bloodshed and fierce rioting in the townships of Alexandra and Daveytown as well as others. The English-speaking white liberal students at the University of the Witwatersrand began marching in show of support in downtown Johannesburg while Soweto burned. We continued to learn while other students died.

'Hey, Ruby.' I felt the sickening stroking of Desmond's fingers on my hair in Miss Radcliffe's geography class. He had moved seats once again, away from Monica, and was, much to my loathing, in his old seat behind me. I tried to ignore him and shift my focus to Miss Radcliffe's lesson.

She wrote the word 'ARGENTINA' on the blackboard. 'Argentina is the second-largest country in South America. Anyone care to guess which is the first?'

Desmond wound a finger round and round a lock of my hair until I felt a painful tug at the roots.

'Ouch. Stop!' I said.

'Desmond and Ruby! I will have to move you again, Desmond, if you two start with your old hanky panky,' she squawked.

'Never got any hanky from this little panky,' he said under his breath, but loud enough for nearby classmates to hear. They all laughed.

'Ruby and Desmond!' Miss Radcliffe rapped her pointing stick on the table. 'I want a ten-page essay from each of you on Argentina's biggest exports.'

'Brazil!' Desmond suddenly blurted out. 'That's the biggest country in South America.' He flashed one of his disarming smiles at her.

'Very good, Desmond,' she said slowly.

'I know, because I've been there twice. Do I still have to do the essay?' he asked playfully.

'Five pages because you knew the answer. But still ten for you!' The tip of her stick pointed like a weapon at me. I looked away. 'I'm talking to you, Miss Winters. And don't think you can ignore the assignment just because you're dropping out of our school in a few weeks.'

There was a general murmur in the classroom and I tried not to look up as I nodded my head that, yes, I did understand.

'Drop out. Traitor,' Desmond taunted me quietly. 'But

187

still the best-looking girl in the school.' He began stroking my hair again and I tried not to flinch.

'It is located between Chile and Uruguay . . .' Miss Radcliffe droned on.

'Monica and I are over,' Desmond leaned forward and whispered. 'She wouldn't put out.'

I tried to pull myself forward on my seat but he grabbed my hair and held it firmly.

'Not so fast,' Desmond chuckled slowly. 'I figured you must be putting out plenty for your big brute *boer*.'

I winced.

'Yeah . . . you are, aren't you? That's okay. Let the Afrikaner *ouk* break you in, do the dirty work. Get you nice and ready for my smooth entry.'

In a flash I was on my feet, my body, my words, no longer in control of their actions. I turned and faced Desmond. 'I would rather die before I would ever let you touch me!'

I didn't care that Miss Radcliffe screamed at the top of her lungs that I would be put in detention for the rest of the term as she hurled her pointed stick at me, nor did I care that everyone in the class sat with open mouths as I lit the final explosion and destroyed what was left of me at Barnard High.

'I'm glad I'm leaving! You are all so bloody spoiled and self-involved!' I stormed from the room as I heard Desmond threaten to have his father stop giving millions to the school if I wasn't expelled immediately.

I did not have a purpose or a direction. I knew I just needed to escape. I walked then ran out of the school building, the cold air filling my lungs as I gained speed. I headed across the manicured lawns, jumping over trimmed garden beds and polished sprinklers. It was as if a shackle had been cut loose from me and I was free to be Ruby Winters, the real me, for the first time at Barnard High.

As I rounded a corner at the furthest end of the school property I almost collided with an overturned wheelbarrow. Its contents lay strewn about, chopped-off heads of dried geraniums, unruly twigs that lay haphazardly about but it was the huddled form of a man on the ground amongst them that stopped me in my tracks. I recognized the wilted flowers on his old hat, the faded blue earth-stained overalls. His whole body shook uncontrollably, his face buried in his lap. I took a small step towards him and touched his heaving shoulder.

'Sir, are you okay?'

He seemed oblivious to my presence so I crouched down beside him. He smelled like freshly cut lawn and damp, rich earth.

'Sophia, Sophia, my Sophia,' he cried.

I patted his shoulder. 'Sir . . .'

He raised his anguished, wrinkled face and stared at me, but it was through me that he looked, to a vision of a little girl, I would soon learn, who lay unmoving on the potholed street. Her homemade sign that read, 'NO AFRIKAANS IN SOWETO!', written neatly in her girlish handwriting, discarded alongside her petite frame.

'Sophia?' I said. 'Sir?'

'She is my only granddaughter. They kill her.' His face

189

contorted in an agonized grimace. Tears ran into the deep lined crevices on his weathered face.

'I am so sorry,' I said, but knew that words like 'sorry' could not dam up even a single tear in his flood of pain. 'You should be with your family.'

'No.' He wiped his face with the back of his stained sleeve. 'Cannot. Must work or lose my job . . .'

'Surely they will understand?'

The old man looked at me closely for the first time. A look of recognition crossed his face.

'You are the girl in the window. The one that wave, yes?' He sniffed.

'Yes.'

'No child here ever say hello to me before. Thirty-two years working at this school and you are the first one.'

My eyes prickled. I knew what it was like to be invisible at Barnard High for a few weeks but thirty-two years seemed intolerable.

'I'm sorry,' I said again, wishing there was a word in the English language that conveyed more than its insufficient sentiment.

'My *umlilewane*, she is ten. She go to school at Phefeni Junior but she will never go again.' The old gardener held his head and shook it back and forth in disbelief. 'My daughter, she call over here to the school and they come and find me in the rose garden to tell me. But I cannot go to Soweto to be with my daughter. It is closed now by the police and I must work . . .'

A large ball of anger filled me. It barrelled down on me like a giant rock as I knelt on the ground beside the broken old man who displayed not an ounce of blame or malice towards the world. A world that had given him a hard, lonely life and had taken away a child that he loved so much, yet all he displayed was sorrow and acceptance.

'I want you to know, sir, that what your granddaughter did was brave and noble and important.' My voice quivered. 'I also want you to know that for all the years I have attended this school, your beautiful gardens have made me happy, especially when I was having a bad day.'

The old man looked at me through dark filmy eyes. 'Sir,' he said slowly. 'No one has ever called me that. It is usually "boy" that I am called.' He lowered his head and bowed. 'Thank you, miss.'

'Ruby,' I said, 'my name is Ruby Winters.' I held out my hand to him and he took it shyly in his rough, weathered palm.

'Benjamin Mpatha.' His mouth turned up slightly at the corners. 'I thank you, Miss Ruby, for showing an old man much kindness on such a sad day.'

'I wish I could do more,' I said.

'You have done enough.' He bowed slightly again.

'I may not be seeing you again, Mr Mpatha,' I said as I stood. 'I'm leaving to attend a different school. Today is probably my last day here.' I looked up at the imposing brick building, the ivy and bougainvillea that climbed the stately walls, the empty, pristine quadrangle and the imposing gates that marked the entrance to our protected, affluent world.

The old man pulled himself up slowly from the ground and dusted off his grimy overalls. 'I will not forget you,

Miss Ruby. Girl that wave from the window.' He took a step towards me.

'I will not forget you either.'

I leaned forward and kissed him quickly on his damp cheek.

He patted my arm as fresh tears sprung in his old eyes. I watched as he shuffled back to his wheelbarrow, bending with some difficulty to straighten it right-side up again.

As I turned to walk away, I felt drawn to look at him one last time before I made my way towards the school gates. Benjamin Mpatha stood amongst all that he tended, the majestic trees, the lush green lawn, the rich variety of seasonal flowers. I watched as he secured the elastic band of his straw hat under his chin, an act that he had done a thousand times and one that he would do a thousand times more. I knew that he would continue to nurture these gardens and keep them beautiful until he could no longer stand on his feeble legs.

He must have felt my gaze, for he looked up and raised his hand slowly to wave at me. I waved back. I willed myself to freeze the moment, the very second, so that I could cherish one last snapshot of the only person that had truly mattered to me at Barnard High, surrounded by the spilled broken twigs and flowers that lay waiting to be gathered up in his gentle old hands.

Chapter Twenty-Seven

The phone in our house did not stop ringing that evening. Mother and Father would alternate jumping up from the dinner table to answer it. There had been only one call earlier in the evening for me, from Johann, who spoke quickly and said that it was very important that we see each other the next day. I tried to get him to tell me what was so pressing but all he said was, 'Tomorrow. Stay safe until then, my love.' I could barely eat the soft mashed potatoes and breaded chicken in front of me. The food stuck in my throat. Blocking its passage was the word 'expelled'.

'Well, looks like Julian's made it out of Johannesburg.' Father returned to the table after a particularly long phone conversation. Mother nodded. I noticed that she too had barely touched her food.

'Good. Let's pray he makes it across the Mozambique border,' she said quietly as she absently swirled her empty fork on her plate.

Father sat down in his seat and, unlike Mother and me, ate with gusto. It was as if the riots and its ripple effect had charged him with new hope and enthusiasm. Gone was the hard, set line of his mouth. He spoke between forkfuls of mashed potato about how the ANC was ready to 'push the envelope' and that change might come about sooner than we had all thought.

'Peace in our time!' He wiped his mouth with a linen napkin. 'Neville Chamberlain, 1938. Do they teach you things like that in school, Ruby?'

I practically jumped at the word 'school'. I shook my head.

'Oh, about school, I almost forgot,' Mother said matter-of-factly with a look that meant she most certainly hadn't. 'Principal Dandridge called the gallery this afternoon looking for me. Apparently a boy named Desmond and his father are demanding that Ruby be expelled.'

Father almost choked on the chicken he was wolfing down. I felt the blood drain from my face and leave my body.

'Relax, David.' Mother put her hand up to calm him while I remained ashen and speechless. 'That pompous boy called our daughter terrible names, turned an entire grade of students against her, had Johann beaten up at the dance and, worse yet, has made it impossible for Ruby to stay at the school. I mentioned all these charming facts to Principal Dandridge but not one word penetrated his fat hide.'

A small defiant smile appeared on Mother's face. 'So I told Principal Dandridge that if he yields to the demands of another parent, who just happens to be the school's biggest financial donor, we would be sure to press charges against that certain ill-bred, ill-mannered boy for trespassing on our property and attempting to accost our daughter some weeks ago.' Mother wiped the corners of her mouth delicately with a napkin and held my gaze. 'I thought that would be okay with you, Ruby,' she said, without altering her tone. 'Snobs hate scandals.'

I reached for her small hand across the table and squeezed it, since words of gratitude could not get past the humiliation and hurt in my throat.

'Should have been a lawyer instead of a gallery owner, Annabel,' Father chuckled. 'Don't worry, Ruby. You'll finish up the term at Barnard – only two more weeks.' Father wiped an errant tear that had escaped from my eye. 'A new beginning for you and perhaps a new beginning for our country,' Father said lightly.

'Let's hope.' Mother sighed. 'Ruby will be fine but I'm afraid there's a long road between here and harmony.' She looked over to the empty chair where Julian used to sit and shook her head. 'I pray he's all right . . .'

But Julian was not all right.

It was Mother's deep, anguished moans that rolled in long, desperate notes that woke me just as the delicate sun began warming the world outside in its frail light. It was a sound that I had never heard from her in all my seventeen years.

'Why? Why? WHY?' she cried. I could hear her fists pounding something hard.

I lay still and looked at the painting, the seagull flying

high over the smokestacks of Soweto, the hopeful boy on the ground gazing upwards, and knew that it was about Julian. I could not get up to find out what had happened. I was not ready for the dreaded truth so I lay there until Father came to give me the news.

'They've got him. Bloody Detective Groenewald and his bastard men!'

At daybreak Father had received a call from a long-trusted underground informer that Julian and sixteen other ANC members had been picked up close to the Mozambique border and were all being held without bail as political prisoners. They were being brought back to Johannesburg to be incarcerated at Diepkloof Prison. They had all been well disguised as migrant workers and were hidden, amongst the livestock, in a closed cattle truck, a means of transport that was rarely searched. But they never stood a chance. The seventeen men and women had been tailed all the way from Johannesburg by an elite team from the Special Branch. The victory, as it was reported in the papers a week later, was all owed to the unwavering per-severance of one determined man on the force. Detective Henrick Groenewald.

Father sat dejectedly on my bed and told me of the cattle truck and the migrant-worker disguises, and I imagined the smirk on Detective Groenewald's face as he pulled Julian from the mooing, manure-filled truck, his icy grey eyes taking in Julian's migrant garb.

'Not quite the reception you're used to, is it, fancy pants

artist boy?' I could imagine him saying as he wiped the cow dung from under his boots on to Julian's trousers.

Father patted my bedcovers then left me to make phone calls to see what he could do for Julian and the other ANC members who had been captured.

I thought back to the first time I met Julian. Had it only been months ago? So much had changed in my life in such a short time.

As I lay there, the sunlight filtering ever brighter through my window, I realized that life was bitter-sweet, good and bad, perfect and imperfect all at once and that our purpose was to survive and thrive at both ends of the spectrum. Something inside me began to form, then like a leaded weight it sank, and kept sinking before settling on my ocean floor. It did not feel heavy and cumbersome. It was an indefinable force inside that made me suddenly feel secured to something larger than anything that might exist in the outside world. For the first time I felt safely anchored to myself.

It was a good thing that this monumental shift in me took place because, had it not, I do not know how I would have survived all that followed.

Mother and Father insisted that I go to school that day even though I was sure the school gates would carry a giant neon sign that flashed, 'NO ENTRANCE, RUBY WINTERS! THE FIRST STUDENT EXPELLED FROM BARNARD HIGH IN TWENTY-FIVE YEARS.'

I made my way begrudgingly through the school gates

where, surprisingly, there was no flashing neon sign announcing my expulsion, but as I alighted from my bike I was immediately approached by Miss Allison, the school administrative assistant, who told me that Principal Dandridge needed to see me in his office right away.

'You may remain here until the end of the term, Ruby, but I think we can both agree that you are no longer a good fit for Barnard High any more than Barnard is a good fit for you.'

'I agree, sir. But I do have one request, sir.'

'What is it?' He drummed his chubby fingers on the polished wooden desk surface, clearly aggravated that I felt I had the right to anything other than a brief reprieve.

'I respectfully request, sir, that Desmond Granger not be allowed to sit in close proximity to me, sir.'

Principal Dandridge sighed and exhaled loudly through his rubbery lips. 'Very well.' He shook a pencil at me. 'But I warn you, Miss Winters, this is the last favour I do for you.'

I wanted to laugh at his choice of words. Keeping Desmond away from me was a necessity, hardly a favour.

At lunch, I wandered through the gardens to look for Benjamin Mpatha, but he was nowhere to be found. I went to Miss Allison in the school office and asked if she knew where he was. She gave me a wilted look and asked what interest it was of mine to enquire after the school gardener.

'He's giving me horticultural advice,' I told her. 'I'm

growing special winter vegetables for a science experiment.'

Satisfied with my ridiculous answer she informed me that he had been given a leave of absence due to a death in the family. I smiled and nodded. A perplexed look crossed her pinched face as I walked away, but it lifted my spirits immeasurably to know that Benjamin was able to be with his daughter to grieve the death of their little Sophia together.

Janice and Clive both looked down at their feet as I passed them in the hallway, but when I sat down in my seat in maths class there was a note with my name on it coiled inside the unused inkwell. I unrolled it quickly and held it out of sight on my lap to read.

Ruby,

I know you probably never want to talk to me again and that's fine 'cause I wasn't a good friend to you but I want you to know that I am sorry about Desmond ruining our friendship and trying to get you expelled. I hope you'll be happier at your new school. Please call me if you ever want to go shopping in Hillbrow on a Saturday just like old times. You have my number.

Monica

I folded the note up neatly and put it into my satchel. I felt numb and strangely detached from her words. The phrase 'old times' was just that. A long, long time ago, or so it seemed. I could scarcely remember all the light-hearted, frivolous fun we used to have. It was all buried under decaying, mildewed piles of damage and disrepair. I knew it was unlikely that I would ever call her again. Desmond was not the cause of our friendship being over. It had been her decision all along.

I spent half the day at school worrying about Julian. Was he being hurt or even tortured? Was he allowed to have visitors soon? I knew that Father was probably building a defence case to try and get him free already. But my insides hurt just thinking about him behind bars.

I longed to be with Johann, to forget about everything just for a few hours. I wanted to feel his arms round me, holding me and making me feel safe. I counted every laborious minute until the last period ended and the school day was over. I raced home as fast as I could and quickly changed out of my school uniform into a white angora sweater and a pair of corduroy trousers. I was about to head out the door and ride to Zoo Lake to meet Johann when the gate buzzer rang.

'It's me, Johann – let me in quick!' His voice sounded frantic through the speaker. My heart pounded as I waited in the driveway for his car to pull up. Within seconds it came to a screeching halt beside me. Johann flung the door open and sprung out. He grabbed me by both arms, a look of panic on his face.

'Ruby, where is your father?' he asked insistently.

'At the office. Johann, you're hurting me!'

He released my arms. 'Call him quickly!'

'I don't understand . . .'

'Listen!' He practically pushed me up the front steps

and I felt my heart leaping wildly like a trapeze artist on the high wire without a net. 'My *pa*, he still has close ties to *Die Broederbond* because of my grandfather's involvement with them. *Die Broederbond*, they work closely with the Special Branch, especially in matters of removing political vermin, as Pa calls them.'

He guided me to the phone in the kitchen, his hand searing into my back like a pointed staff.

'Johann, what are you saying?'

He pulled the receiver off the wall and put it to my ear.

'Call your father now! Tell him they are planning on ambushing him on his way home tonight. He will not even make it to see the inside of a jail cell!'

'Johann?'

'Call!' His eyes were wild.

I held his gaze and with trembling fingers dialled my father on his private line that only Mother and I and his underground political contacts knew.

'Daddy, it's me, Ruby.' I could barely speak. 'Johann needs me to tell you something . . .' I took a deep breath and tried to finish the sentence but no words came out.

Johann grabbed the phone from me.

'*Meneer*, sir, please listen to me. Your life is in danger. I have overheard my father say on the phone last night to someone that the little English *meisie* that his son was dating will be minus a father soon. I called Ruby to meet with her today to tell her this but this afternoon I come home from school and my father is dead drunk on the couch and he laughs and tells me that I am a fool to have fallen in love with the daughter of a political troublemaker and that he was glad he forbid me to see her any more. He laughed even harder and then said that the boys from *Die Broederbond* were going to kill the "kaffir-loving lawyer" tonight before the police even have a chance to arrest him tomorrow.'

My father must have said something to Johann because he paused for a second and shook his head.

'Sir, I am here to tell you to leave. Time is running out and I fear for you. I beg you . . .'

I looked around the kitchen. The antique copper pots that were strung like gleaming lanterns from above that Mother and I had hung just two summers ago. They had been a gift from a lesbian artist who had wanted to show her gratitude to Mother for allowing her to exhibit her rather sexually explicit works that no other gallery would show. Each pot was inscribed with a word that reflected how she felt about Mother. *Radical. Courageous. Spirited. Beauty. Rule breaker.*

Now the rules that they broke were the weapons that could kill my father.

'Thank you, sir. It has been a pleasure knowing you.'

Johann handed the phone back to me then put his arm round me. I leaned against him for support.

'Yes, Daddy,' I whispered.

'Ruby, listen.' He sounded calm but I could feel the tension behind his words. 'Pack as much as you can, but not too much.' Father took a deep breath before continuing, 'I had heard that they would be coming for me, but I thought I had more time.'

'Mother?' I said with mounting fear.

'I'm calling her now. Start packing. I'll be home soon.'

'Okay,' was all I could get out.

'Tell Johann he must leave our house right away. Not safe. Lock all the doors and don't let anyone in after he leaves.' Before he hung up Father hastily added, 'Ruby. I forgot to thank him. He may well have saved my life.'

Chapter Twenty-Eight

How did I say goodbye to Johann, to my house, to my life and all that was familiar to me in just the blink of an eye? It was almost that fast. My seventeen years of life in Johannesburg, South Africa, ended just like that.

I know I held on to Johann and we both cried and we swore that we would see each other again. We said that space and time would not alter how we felt no matter how far we were from each other or how long we were apart. I know I said a tearfully quick goodbye to Loretta on the phone and that we both thanked the stars above that we had met and had become friends so fast, as if we somehow knew that time was running out. I did not have the chance to hug Uncle D or Thandi goodbye. There simply wasn't time. But the hardest person that I had to say goodbye to was the one I least expected to ever be separated from in my life.

I locked the doors after Johann had left and ran on petrified legs upstairs to hastily begin packing. I did not have a moment to think about what clothes meant more to me and what hairclips and earrings I would want. I threw a pair of shoes, a scarf, two pairs of trousers, a few tops and a jacket into a small duffle bag and toiletries into a small plastic zipper one. These were all just items that mattered not one bit, essentials to clothe me and keep me clean on the road ahead. But there was one thing I knew that I would not leave behind. I needed it to be with me every step of the journey into the unknown.

I carefully lifted the heavy frame from the wall and pried the glass off the picture with scissors. I gently removed its backing and held the painting naked and raw in my hands. The colours were even more vivid without the frame and glass casing round it and the crayon shimmered ever brighter in the little boy's hand.

'I'm taking you with me,' I told him softly as tears spilled down my cheeks. I rolled the painting up tenderly and tied a blue ribbon round it to keep it secure. That was all I took with me when some hours later we left under cover of dark into the cold night air.

I heard the screeching of tyres as Mother's champagne Jaguar roared up the driveway. Father's Citroën followed just a few seconds behind her. I watched from my bedroom window as they climbed the stairs hastily together. I ran to them as Father opened the front door. We held each other ever so tightly, our little circle of three. We stood that way for a few seconds before Mother, blotchy faced and eyes rimmed red, stepped out of the circle.

'Come,' she said softly. 'I need to tell you both something.'

Father and I followed her into the living room. 'We don't have much time, my darling Ruby, my beloved David.' Her face searched ours back and forth. Her hands flitted from the pulse in her neck to errant wisps of hair that strayed across her cheeks.

'We are such an extraordinary family, aren't we?' Her voice was taut with emotion. 'And you know how much I love you both?' Her eyes searched deep into mine and then into Father's, who with his steady hand traced Mother's delicate jawbone.

'Yes, Annabel.' I could almost feel his pain, filled with immeasurable love, which floated towards her.

'And you both know, don't you, that my life's work is to help artists.' She held Father's fingers in hers while she reached for mine with her free hand. She closed her eyes and tilted her head backwards. 'Dear God, give me the strength to do this.' She lowered her head and opened her eyes, flooded with tears. 'I'm not coming with you.'

I felt my feet lift from the ground as she spoke.

'I can't abandon my artists when they need me the most. Kumalo, Joshua Sisweakne, Makala and now Julian. I will not walk away from all I have worked so hard to give them. Dignity, respect, walls on which to hang their beautiful works, hope, yes, above all, hope, that one day every gallery in South Africa will proudly display their art. They are as much a part of my life as you both are.'

Father bowed his head but held on to Mother's hand and kissed her palm over and over again. 'I understand. I know,' was all he said.

Mother pulled me towards her and I burrowed myself into her tangerine scent and her soft pale skin.

'Mommy!' I cried. 'Mommy!'

She held on to me and wept.

Father went upstairs to quickly pack and make a phone call to his underground friends who would take us out of Johannesburg. Mother and I sat on the couch clinging to each other. She stroked my hair over and over again.

'It is still safe for me to be here, you know that. Don't worry about me. I'll be fine. It's your father they are after. But you must go with him, Ruby. He must take you away from this country filled with hate and fear. I will come, I promise. I will follow when the time is right.' She managed to get out between deep sobs.

'Julian . . .' I sniffed. 'Will you see him, Mother, and say goodbye from me?'

'I will, my darling child, I will.'

'How long will he be in jail for, Mother?'

'No one knows, but I will do everything I can to get him free.'

She laid her cheek against mine and rocked me back and forth, just as she did when I was a little child. She sang a half-Xhosa, half-English lullaby that she would sometimes sing to put me to sleep. How could either of us ever have known that its lyrics would come to pass?

'Thulatu thula, baba, thula sana, though your mommy's gone it's not forever.
Rest your weary head now, baby, don't you cry.

When the sun goes down and it is time to sleep
She will come to you as if in a dream.
Thula, baba, thula sana. Thula, baba, thula sana.'

Within a few hours Father and I sneaked out of our house and were on our way out of the city that had brought me so much love and so much pain.

'*Egoli.*' Father held my hand as we walked with our bags down the back lane that ran beside our house. 'City of gold.' Then he added sadly, 'We shall miss you.' It was as if he were reading my mind.

We were picked up several blocks from Westcliff Drive by a large black man, who flashed his lights at us in a special sequence that Father had been given as 'the sign'. The man said nothing as we climbed into the back of his non-descript van. We travelled on lumpy seats, where the spring coils bit into my flesh like angry ants. We breathed in the unpleasant aroma of stale fish and chips for many hours before stopping on the outskirts of a small mining town near Nelspruit.

In a dimly lit shanty hut I was given a blonde wig and a scratchy petticoat-lined dress that was a size too small for me by a young militant-looking black woman. She handed Father a bag of items. He carefully taped on the black beard and moustache. Then the woman took out a razor and quickly shaved Father's head bald. She motioned for me to stand against the peeling shanty wall and told me to smile as she snapped a Polaroid picture. I was dazed and hungry and tired but she urged me to say cheese to get the necessary photograph. While the pictures were drying she took a smiling snap of Father, who was now hardly recognizable. After a few minutes she pasted the photos into two passports and handed them to Father. We were now Mike and Veronica Seagram a father and daughter from Germiston travelling into Mozambique for a brief holiday. The woman even handed me a piece of paper that was signed by the principal of Germiston High giving me, Veronica Seagram, permission to miss a few days of school.

'Great bit of forgery,' Father complimented the grim woman, who nodded her head and ushered us back into the van with a loaf of bread and a flask of hot tea. I was grateful to have something warm in my stomach and once I was done eating I put my head on Father's shoulder and quickly fell asleep.

I dream that Benjamin and Thandi are getting married and Sophia, carrying her sign to keep Afrikaans out of the schools, is the flower girl. With a prefect badge gleaming on my school uniform, I am the bridesmaid. I dream that Julian sits at an easel and sketches us with a purple crayon while Mother and Father dance close, their arms wrapped tightly round each other. Then Johann walks towards me and waves. 'Girl in the window' waves back. He pulls his oars up to come to me.

Father shook me gently, 'Border is up ahead, Ruby. I mean, Veronica.'

Mozambique had, the year before, become an independent country after years of being under Portuguese rule. The new government, now under a black ruler, gave shelter to South African ANC members and supporters. Father explained this to me in hushed tones as we neared the guard gate. I could hear our mostly silent driver speak rapidly now to the uniformed guard in a foreign language, which must have been Portuguese since Father said it was still the most spoken language of the country.

'Stay calm,' Father said quickly, just as the back door of the van was thrown open by a dark-eyed man. He indicated for us to give him our papers. He glanced over them and looked closely at the pictures in the passports, then examined Father and me. He fingered the forged principal's letter and squinted at the words on the document. I could barely breathe and I could feel Father's leg muscles tighten on the seat beside me. Neither of us moved. After a few excruciatingly tense seconds the man nodded his head and handed Father back the papers. He made a signal to the driver that we could move through the border gates. Father put the documents back into his jacket pocket slowly then reached for my hand and squeezed it but kept his eyes fixed on the road ahead. The road that would lead us to Maputo, the newly named capital. Had Father turned to look at me he would have seen the tears that fell, filled with memory of fresh summer rains, mint and lavender in the garden, winding bike rides down Westcliff Ridge, rowing on Zoo Lake. I longed for my mother's small hand to be brushing a strand of errant hair from my eyes, I yearned to breathe in the paint fumes of the studio while Julian's deep voice explained a particular painting to me. I ached to feel Johann's strong arms round me and to hear Loretta's sweet voice telling me that I was her friend, no matter what. My heart heaved just as we hit a large bump, the first of many on the badly made roads to Maputo.

'America,' Father said to me the next morning after a bad night of sleep in a cramped hotel room in the industrial part of the city. Outside I could hear the grinding of machinery and the hissing of steam being released from a nearby combustion plant. 'We can't waste any time. I spoke to your mother this morning and she's locking up the house and going to Cape Town for a while. Much too risky for her to be in Johannesburg right now.'

Father's shaved head now had a dark shadow covering it. I knew that in just a few weeks his hair would grow back and be thick and wavy again but nothing else in our lives would ever be the same again.

'America, Father? Whereabouts?' I pulled the blonde wig back on to my head and prayed that I would not have to wear it once we were far across the Atlantic Ocean.

'New York,' he said. 'My contacts have a place for us to stay there.'

Father sat down on the edge of the small twin bed and ran his hand along the frayed bedspread. 'I would have stuck to corporate law and left politics alone –' he shook his head – 'had I known it would do this to us. To you, Ruby.'

'Father, stop!' I raised my voice. 'You've saved people's lives, freed them from jail when they were innocent. Stood up for what you believed in.' I took his hand in mine.

'*Alles moet verby gaan*, Daddy. That's what Loretta says. Everything shall pass.'

'How did I get so lucky? To have two such remarkable women in my life?' He pulled me towards him and I could feel his heart beating in his anguished chest.

It was a large plane and not a small seagull that carried us high above the continent of Africa, still it soared ever higher away from all that was familiar into the blue skies.

On the plane I wrote a long, mushy, sad letter to Johann and promised that I would write in a few days once we were settled in New York. I remembered a poem from school about a brave warrior and wrote it on a card for Julian hoping that it would find its way to him through Mother. The events of the past few days made me feel suddenly very tired and I leaned against Father, who was in the seat beside me, and dozed off. My last thought drifting off was that I prayed when I awoke I would be home and in my own bed; the sunlight filtering through my flimsy curtains, the welcome sound of Mother's slippers pattering across the carpeted floor with a cup of warm tea for me. But I awoke to the humming of the plane's engines.

I held on to Father's arm and he covered my hand with his.

'Everything's going to be all right, Ruby.'

'Will it, Father?' I asked.

Eighteen hours later we landed in America.

Chapter Twenty-Nine

On the fourth of July I stood in the middle of Times Square with thousands of people to celebrate America's bicentenary. Most were dressed in red, white and blue and many wore the fashions and styles from the eighteenth century. The American flag was hoisted on every building and national flags of all sizes were waved in the hands of children and adults alike. I stood beside Father, whose hair already covered his head in short bristles, and our new housemate, Ezekiel, an ANC member now living in exile in Brooklyn.

'Two hundred years of freedom. Liberty and justice for all!' the crowd yelled.

Had it been not even three weeks since the Soweto Riots? Had I already been in New York for a fortnight? Time had taken on a different pace, fast and slow, moments that felt like hours, and hours that passed like seconds. Everything came and went in strange collections of time and space. I still had to catch up inside with the rapid changes that had occurred in my life. The lack of routine, the unknown future that was mine. There was a time, not so long ago, I thought as I watched the sky darken overhead, when I woke up in the morning, got dressed and rode my bike to school. I stopped by my mother's gallery in the afternoons, did my homework, spent time with Julian and ate dinner with my family. It was a time I would never have again.

'It's going to be spectacular!' Ezekiel said excitedly to Father and me. He had lost an arm when he had been placed in solitary confinement in a prison in Pretoria before they released him due to lack of evidence. A white lawyer, not unlike Father, had represented him and found him safe passage to New York six months ago. 'We'll never see anything like this again!' His empty sleeve hung limply by his side as he waved a small flag in his good hand.

There were people of every race and colour melded together: black, white, Hispanic, Germanic, Latino, Asian, Polish, Indian, Russian and more. They held hands, hugged each other, swayed together in unison as the American National Anthem played from loudspeakers that hung all around. Father gazed down at me. His eyes looked tired, the lines etched deeper in his forehead.

'You like fireworks, don't you, Ruby?'

I nodded just as the first explosion of glittering colour filled the night sky. It was followed by another explosive display, then another and another. The immense crowd applauded louder and louder with each new colourful burst of light. It was, just as Ezekiel had predicted, spectacular. Red, white and blue rainbows arced against the backdrop of New York's skyline, fountains of silver poured like shimmering water from the heavens above, crimson and indigo stars exploded everywhere. It was in that moment, when the sky was filled with an overwhelming abundance of colour and light, that I loosened my grasp on the rolled-up object I held so safely in my hand. I undid the ribbon carefully as a fountain of golden light showered down from above. I unfurled its sturdy paper slowly until it lay open against the wide arched rainbows and the glittering stars.

We were thousands of miles away from home, but I held the picture of the hopeful young boy from the shanty towns of Soweto, his tattered clothes two sizes too big, up towards the light, the purple crayon glowing ever brighter in his little hand.

'Look, Julian,' I whispered, 'I have brought you with me to freedom.'

Author's Note

The Soweto Riots have been seen by many as the event that signalled the beginning of the end of apartheid. The effects of the Soweto Riots were echoed across South Africa and the world.

The South African government, as an immediate aftermath of the Afrikaans language issue, which was the igniting cause of the Soweto Riots, withdrew the Afrikaans language requirement for black schoolchildren.

The 1980s were turbulent and bloody, but it was becoming clear that the era of apartheid was nearing its end.

On 10 February 1990, the headline of every newspaper around the world was that South Africa's most famous political prisoner, Nelson Mandela, was released from prison. Hundreds of other black political prisoners were also released. They included well-known black artists who had been incarcerated.

Finally, in 1994 the system of apartheid was dismantled in South Africa forever.

Acknowledgements

My gratitude goes first to my brilliant and very under-standing editor, Sarah Hughes, who encouraged me through a difficult personal year in her calm, gentle way and whose notes are always spot-on. A big thanks to my copy editors, Samantha Mackintosh and Wendy Tse, for their tireless and meticulous work, and an additional word of thanks to Publicity Director Adele Minchin, who takes such good care of me when I am in the UK.

My deep appreciation goes to my wonderful agent, Shana Kelly at the William Morris Agency, who works so very hard on my behalf and keeps me focused and sane. My gratitude also goes to agents Tracy Fisher and Alicia Gordon who both take such a personal interest in my life and career.

My creative process is never a solitary one and I am blessed to have a wonderful family and group of friends who are so supportive of my writing life. Thanks to my father, Harold, who is my sounding board and encyclopedia for anything historically South African, and to my mother, a voracious reader, whose opinion I truly value. Thanks and love forever to my big sister, Caron, who is my rock and strength in life.

A special thanks to ex-husband Marvin Katz, who remains such an important part of my life, and a big kiss to stepdaughter Vickie Espudo and granddaughter Emma J. A million words of gratitude must also go to the extra-ordinarily talented women in my writing group, Terri Cheney (friend extraordinaire), Helena Kriel (South African soul sister) and Terry Hoffmann, led by great friend, mentor and author, Lisa Doctor. Our Tuesday nights truly are sacred.

An eternal thanks to my best friend, Kathy Jackoway, who has held my hand for twenty years. My love and gratitude goes to friend of many years Barbara Mandel who is there for me in so many ways, especially when life is less than perfect. Thank you, my dedicated animal-rescue partner, Sylva Kelegian, for sharing my struggles and joys on a daily basis in our efforts to save animals in crisis. What a great year of saving dogs (and a few cats) this has been for us! Thanks, as always, to Dr Ron Furst for his unwavering support of me, and his never-ending generosity. A word of appreciation to Damon Shalit who shares my passion for bringing stories of the country of our birth into the light. My love goes to Patty Wheelock for being such a good friend and wonderful human being. My gratitude to my dear friend Andrea Kerzner who is a reminder of how much we have both grown since our high-school days in Johannesburg.

A very, very special thanks goes to cousin Linda Givon, owner of the Goodman Gallery in Johannesburg and Cape Town, South Africa, for being the inspiration behind the story of an art-gallery owner whose devotion and commitment to helping black artists during the reign of apartheid was unequalled. The wealth of information that you shared with me about your experiences was invaluable.

Lastly, a big hug goes to my beautiful eighteen-year-old daughter, Jordan, who is always willing to give me her creative input (even in the early hours of the morning) and whose insights truly helped shape some of the ideas in this novel.